Praise for *Jeanne*

"Sexy, sad, super smart. Written with a translator's complicated love of language and a flâneur's understanding that one can never go home. I loved this sleek and adventurous book."

Lindsay Lerman

"A fastidious eye and compelling style provides an open window onto the bewildering mirror puzzle of an array of rapture and rancour, the markers of which include Lizzy Mercier Descloux, strap-on-luv, Anne-Marie Alonzo, Simone de Beauvoir, Masculin/Féminin et al."

Richard Cabut

Arielle Burgdorf

JEANNE

MOIST

First published in 2025 by MOIST

Arielle Burgdorf's novella *Prétend* was published by End of the Line Press, Canada, in 2024. Large sections of this work, or versions of them, also appear in *Jeanne*. They are reprinted here with their permission.

https://www.moistbooks.com

ISBN: 978-1-913430-19-1

Cover image © Nastassja Simensky & Hugh Nicholson, 2024.

A catalogue record for this book is available from the British Library.

Dedicated to the people of Montréal

I. Trouble

In Montreal, Jean comes undone.

Shuffling between borders, currencies, and time zones, countless imaginary markers she doesn't believe in, the old Jean dissolves. She slips, she becomes slippage, slippery. The markers blur and blur until finally they blur the very silhouette of self. When everything breaks down, what is left of her? She is not sure.

Bored in her aeroplane seat, ass numb, she anxiously waits to get off. She tugs at the black thread unravelling on one side of her jeans. She can't stop pulling as it grows longer and longer, until finally, in one violent movement, she rips it free of the denim. Afterwards she goes through customs, casually sidestepping the question of business or pleasure — it is always a bit of both. She enters the terminal, the fakely cheerful red Tim Hortons sign alerting her that she is home. *Toujours frais.*

Somewhere in the terminal, Jean becomes Jeanne. The pronunciation of her name shifts from *gene* to something closer to *john* or *jeune*, depending on who is saying it. She trades Montreal for Montréal, Dunkin for Tims, Speedway for Couche-Tard, corner store for dépanneur, and fuck for her grandfather's expression: *crisse de câlisse de tabarnak d'esti de sacrament.* That one makes her smile. Nothing comes close to the Québécois art of swearing.

She is home, but this isn't really her home. She hasn't been to Montréal in years. Although she was born here, she is forever an outsider. If home means a place you belong, a place you are understood without having to explain yourself, then no, Jeanne does not have a home. She has no mother tongue; her mother is dead and her father is missing. She is not a citizen of anywhere in particular.

Jeanne orders a cup of black coffee from Tims that she drinks on the curb outside while smoking her first cigarette of the day. The coffee is way too hot, scraping a layer of skin off her tongue. The cigarette is perfect.

*

That afternoon, she wanders Boulevard St. Laurent, known by some old-timers as the Main, searching for a café where she can write. Jeanne is a translator — well, she's trying to be a translator. She is here, in Montréal, for a translation job that she is not sure will come through. Part of her is convinced the whole thing is a scam, a sadistic joke, that there was no job for her to begin with. But she is used to taking on any translation projects that come her way, and this one pays particularly well.

Her obsession with translation springs from growing up between and around, circling many cultures, many languages. And perhaps, she has something to prove. To show she knows her languages inside and out. Even when she is not sure she does. Even when she is not sure anyone can ever know a language so intimately. She is trying to recover her roots, to understand her absent parents through her work. She believes the role of a translator is sacred, somewhere between conspirator and midwife.

But recently, translation feels more like revealing the magic trick behind a precious word, making it vulnerable. Vulnerable to what, or rather who, she is not sure. She's started writing footnotes paragraphs long, explaining the entire cultural context behind a short phrase. Her translator's notes are longer than the original pieces. She knows, of course, that this is unacceptable. Someone paying for a translation of a certified legal document does not want a history of Québécois linguistics. But Jeanne feels possessed. Compelled to write these notes, if only to herself, confined to the margins.

Of course, Jeanne is not just a translator. Most of her income comes from writing essays on French and Russian literature for rich college students. She knows it's wrong, but she can't make a living on translation alone, especially when so many people think she ought to do it for free, out of the goodness of her heart.

Jeanne turns down one street and runs into a flurry of bookshops. She lingers over the bright, geometrically-pleasing displays made by graphic design students, recalling the visceral French term for window-shopping: lèche-vitrine. Window licking. She imagines pressing her nose and mouth against the glass, like a pane of ice, running her tongue along the cold surface. Licking it clean as a dinner plate, horrifying shoppers within.

She settles on a café called Le Hibou, mostly because she likes the blue stained-glass lamps in the window and the collection of owl trinkets inside, like sitting in someone's living room. She orders a chocolatine, her childhood favourite. Her phone buzzes, but she ignores it. Jean would've answered it right away, but Jeanne can't be bothered.

Instead she opens her laptop, continuing an essay on *Candide*. What did Pangloss mean by "Il faut cultiver notre jardin?" She has some fun with it. She brings in the French Enlightenment and Voltaire deep cuts like *La Princesse de Babylone*. Lastly, she sprinkles in a few typos for authenticity. Satisfied, she sends the file back to the student, then fully intends to start translating text for a video game website but does not. Instead, she observes the street outside, imagining Georges Perec in La Place Saint-Sulpice, writing *Tentative d'épuisement d'un lieu parisien*. She loves picturing Perec with his wild hair and impish smile, sitting in cafés, recording field notes on the so-called unremarkable parts of life: the passing of bus routes, items people carried in their hands, flight pathways of pigeons. Jeanne does the same now, watches other selves and finds herself in their actions. On her laptop, she types:

1. An elderly hound dog slumps along the sidewalk. Spotting a grey squirrel, he jolts to life, viciously spirited in his chase. I am surprised to find myself rooting for him, for murder.

2. A young male-female couple holding hands collide into a single man because they refuse to let go of their grip.

3. A woman in a red mini skirt and white high heels ignores a drunken catcaller. He tries first in English, then in French, raising his voice each time. Of course, language is not the problem. Plotte! Salope! uttered at a growl is comprehensible by anyone.

Eventually, the evening soaks in the pale light and the street outside grows dark. She notices a young woman in the back corner of the café looking at her over her cup of coffee. Their eyes connect, lingering a little too long. Then the girl leans her head towards the door, an offer — should we get out of here? Jeanne nods.

They should.

On the curb, they share a cigarette. The other girl introduces herself in French as Violette. She wears her long black hair in a braid that ends just above her ass. Jeanne asks if she's heard of a writer named Violette Leduc. No, she hasn't.

I don't care for books, Violette says proudly, J'aime danser. And then she grins, slyly slipping an arm around Jeanne's waist. Quick as that, they are linked. Jeanne smiles, and leans back against her shoulder, relieved there is no ambiguity. They are going to fuck tonight; it is only a question of when.

Violette leads Jeanne through the dark streets to a basement down a narrow set of stairs. Flashes of red light and smoke pour out of the doorway, and for a second Jeanne has the dizzying sensation of walking into the mouth of Hell. But then she hears music and realises it is a club. The DJ is playing a song Jeanne recognizes, "Herpes Simplex" by Rosa Yemen, who is also Lizzy Mercier Descloux. Descloux screams in a heavy accent towards a crowd of apathetic art school students, as though she is trying to reach through time and shake them out of their complacency. *Méta. Métabolisme. Fuck you. Fuck you. Fuck you. Désolée, désolée!* Jeanne wants to tell Violette she knows this song, but she is afraid with all the noise she will think she's telling her she has herpes, so she says nothing. She is impressed with the club, though. The music is better than expected, though the people are less good-looking. She hides her suitcase in a dimly lit corner, and they head to the dance floor.

Soon they are moving together in the near-darkness. Shadow patterns, shifting tattoos on their bodies. Violette is wearing a shiny, sheer dark blue top, and Jeanne can see her nipples through the fabric. She stops thinking and knocks back shots of bottom-shelf whiskey until her skin is on fire. She wants to hurt her brain. To turn off the spout of language. She is too old to be acting like this, but doesn't care. Violette grabs her and kisses hard, pushes her hands through Jeanne's short hair, fingers running over her skull. They pull even closer, trying to merge. She sweats out words. Rhythm. The record skips, stuttering. More friction. Jeanne keeps trying to place Violette's perfume. Nectarines, and something mysterious. A buzz: Jeanne's phone glows blue in the black. Violette goes to the bathroom and brings back some pills when she returns. Jeanne hasn't done ecstasy in forever. But tonight, she'd like to be ecstatic. She doesn't think it's kicking in, and then suddenly the air around her feels charged, every movement a kind of rapture. Normally, she'd go dance with someone else to avoid seeming clingy, but the e overrules her self-respect. Jeanne gets silly, romantic. Wrapped in fantasy, she believes in the possibility of love.

Méta. Métabolisme. Fuck me. Fuck me. Fuck me. Désolée, désolée!

They leave, stumbling drunk-high, wandering past the late-night takeout places, and her favourite old sign that reads: Super Sexe in bright red, the letters surrounded by surreal images of women in lingerie and capes flying around a blue sky. Further on, warm pink and yellow neon lights that read: Sexothèque. Salons privés. Sexothèque, a word with no satisfying English equivalent, Jeanne thinks. Some leftover relic from the '80s, something you would only cry out in a coke-induced mania: *take me to the sexothèque!* Jeanne wants to peek inside, but Violette pulls her along, her grip surprisingly strong. Down an alleyway, towards a spiral staircase covered in green vines, until they stop outside a large open window. They climb in, and there's a loud crash as Jeanne throws her suitcase onto the floor. Violette whispers: she shares this apartment with five roommates and a cat; hopefully most of them are asleep.

Violette's bedroom is chaotic, possessions splattered everywhere. On the floor, there's a blue vase with white flowers filled with dead stems. She has all these crude drawings framed on the walls, and Jeanne can't tell if they were made by children or by famous artists trying to make art that looks like it came from children. Violette shoves a pile of clothes onto the floor so they have space on the bed. Jeanne is thankful for drugs; if she was more present, she would start to fully register the sour smell, the dirty underwear, the mould on the ceiling. She tells herself she is dreaming. Violette lights a votive candle perilously close to a stack of magazines. Her carelessness is so intense and repetitive it almost seems intentional. Jeanne's cell phone buzzes again, and instead of answering, she buries it under a pillow.

From a drawer, Violette pulls out a large, dark red dildo and a black leather harness with an imprint of a lion's face on it. After some adjustments, she manages to get both the harness and the dildo in the right position. She ties Jeanne to the bed frame with some scarves and fucks her, hard and fast. With one hand Violette teases Jeanne's clit, making her delirious. None of it feels real. Because of the e, every sensation hits just a fraction of a second off. She finds it hard to come and soon gives up. Violette stops to readjust. She bites Jeanne's neck, pour faire des sucettes. Then she presses a smooth hand over Jeanne's mouth, and Jeanne kisses it or thinks she is kissing it but is not sure. She is not allowed to do much else, which is fine because her reactions are sluggish. She is floating, watching their scene as a film in a dark theatre. Violette shrieks when she comes, shaking until her breathing abruptly stops.

In the end, it's all a bit disappointing. After a night of tension and buildup, Violette only seems to care about herself. Outside of the dance floor, she isn't one for conversation. Jeanne mutters that she's hungry, hoping Violette will make them whatever meal is appropriate at this hour. In her torn underwear, she disappears into the kitchen and returns with a half-eaten bag of ketchup chips which she throws at Jeanne. Only then does it occur to Jeanne that she can just leave. She grabs her phone from under the pillow, fetches her suitcase, and heads out without a word to Violette.

On the fire escape, Jeanne finally checks her phone. The screen is lit up blue again: twelve missed calls and a flood of texts, all from the same number and not the number she wants. A fresh message flashes on the screen:

> What the fuck Jean?
> Why aren't you answering?

Her husband.

II. How it Happened

When Jean was younger, she took all the money she'd saved from waitressing and blew it on a plane ticket to Iceland. It was her first time travelling beyond North America, and from the plane, everything looked lush with possibility. Lush, until she realised Reykjavik was incredibly expensive. Even the most modest hotels and restaurants went far beyond her budget. Every golden, poster tourist fantasy she'd been promised — the Blue Lagoon, waterfalls, black lava, Aurora Borealis, the sturdy little ponies — out of reach. Her first few days were miserable, trapped in the hostel where she'd agreed to work in exchange for a bed. She scooped bowls of granola, washed dishes, scrubbed toilets, and answered questions from violent couples arguing their way through backpacking trips.

In her spare time, she went to the library and read for hours because it was the only free place she could think of. The building was very modern, a Nordic paradise of rectangular glass windows, clean lines, minimalist furniture. She felt as if she'd stepped inside a design catalogue.

Alone for hours, Jean obsessed over the Icelandic language, Íslanka. She couldn't cobble together much, but the characters alone were works of art. In English, she read about the history of the island. Íslanka was ancient; you could still hear traces of saltwater and arctic thyme in its rhythm. Young Icelanders could read texts from the very beginning of their country with little trouble. Íslanka transcended time, embracing past, present, future.

On the guest computers she searched for art installations in Iceland, hoping there might be some she could visit. She was excited to find that her favourite poet, Anne Carson, was the writer-in-residence at Vatnasafn in 2008. Vatnasafn was an art space two and a half-hours away from Reykjavik, created by the American artist Roni Horn. It housed a collection of melted glacier water contained in twenty-four slim glass tubes. The website described it as "The Library of Water."

Jean clicked on the photos and zoomed in on the water. Grey pixels filled her screen. She imagined how the shape and colour of liquid would change based on the season and time of day, the light refracting, so that every visitor might experience it differently. But the more she looked, the stronger the urge came on to destroy the imprisoned columns of water. She was surprised at this current of violence welling up in her. Images of broken glass flooded her thoughts.

A loudspeaker announced the library was closing in thirty minutes, first in Íslanka, then in English. Jean wanted to check out a book called *The*

Blue Fox, but the librarian informed her that she would need to be a resident in order to do this.

Please. I'll bring it back in a few days, I promise, Jean begged. The librarian laughed.

You know how many times I've heard that one? she said. We're not a charity.

Jean was about to put the book back, when a solution appeared behind her in line. His name was Jökull. Wordlessly, he took her book and added it to his own pile of DVDs.

Outside, she thanked him. He waved her off.

It's nothing, he said. He started to ask where she was from, what she was doing here, did she have a boyfriend. She felt obliged to answer but eyed him warily. He was the kind of person many people found handsome, tall and thin like a Dane, with an asymmetrical haircut and green-edged glasses, very hip. But she did not find him handsome; his personality was too aggressive. When she mentioned the arrangement at the hostel, Jökull interrupted her.

Fuck the hostel, he said. You're staying with me. He started to walk and motioned for her to follow. Jean wasn't sure she wanted to stay with him, but Jökull was right. The thought of going back to the hostel was unbearable.

Jökull lived near the centre of the city in a compact but mostly clean flat. He had a TV, a small kitchen, a bookshelf, an expensive bike propped against one wall, and a foldout couch where he hosted visitors from time to time. There was also, he offered, his bedroom. Jean shook her head. The couch is great, she smiled.

There was a German girl staying there too, curvy and rosy-cheeked, with golden curls. Her name was Annaliese, but Jean kept almost calling her Heidi because she reminded her of the book. Annaliese had spent the wretched winter months working on various sheep farms.

Now, she explained, I want to fuck and party. She was always drinking white wine and laughing, no matter the time of day. Jean liked her immediately, and because of her, decided to stay the night. They spent the evening warm and drunk, telling stories and showing each other pop songs until Jökull pulled out an acoustic guitar and ruined everything.

*

In the morning, Jökull went off to his job at a coffee shop down the street. Jean was a little surprised he had a real job; everyone she'd met in Reykjavik so far had jobs like being a DJ or graffiti artist. At first, she wasn't sure what to do with herself, but since Annaliese also had no money or plans, she convinced her they should hitchhike to Strokkur, the famous geyser. Her first choice was Vatnasafn, but it was too far and only open for a few hours every day. Jean had seen photos of Strokkur in a brochure, impressed by the immense spray arching up like a spire. She was dying to see it in real life.

The morning they left was cloudy and grey, threatening a storm. They split a pack of chocolate-covered raisins stolen from a gas station and waited in the spitting rain for someone to take pity on them. After an hour, a man stopped, but he didn't take them very far. They had to find a few more rides, and Jean got to use the few Íslanka phrases she remembered, but mostly the drivers wanted to talk to Annaliese about the intricacies of birthing lambs, the réttir, and whether you needed an Icelandic sheepdog or if other breeds might work just as well. Eventually, they made it to Strokkur. The tourists who had taken the official bus stared at them in confusion, like they were wild elves who had appeared out of nowhere. In thick mud, they stood and watched the water bubble up. It looked nothing like the photos. Jean scolded herself for being disappointed in nature. Why did humans always need everything to be giant in order to be awed?

An article she'd read at the Reykjavik library came to mind. An artist called Marcus Evaristti had once dyed the geyser pink with fruit juice. Icelanders were furious; they arrested and fined him for obstructing nature. Jean sympathised with the Icelanders' point of view. Artists seemed to think of Iceland as their personal canvas. They praised what they saw as Iceland's purity and untouchedness as if those were neutral concepts. They found the terrain irresistible; a whole island of white noise, deep valleys, snowy tundras. They especially loved the whiteness.

Jean remembered the Library of Water. A way of bringing order to the overwhelming unknown. Was Roni Horn preserving truth or obscuring it with her own narrative? She wasn't sure.

On the one hand, she saw Evaristti dyeing the geyser as just another attempt at land domination, a territorial pissing. Secretly, a way of coping with his own fear at the immensity of nature. The ultimate hubris, to think one could "improve" the natural world. And yet.

She had to admit that his pink geyser installation was one of the most breathtaking things she'd ever seen, even with the shitty resolution. A burst of pink light exploding across a striking blue sky. Pining for the heavens, a soft pink cloud returning home. Pour Jean, ce sont des images poétiques, étrangement naturelles.

She had seen plenty of fountains dyed hot pink for Breast Cancer awareness or neon green for St. Patrick's Day. But this was different. A subtler shade of artificial. Evaristti's geyser gestured towards nature, the pink hues of sunset. If not exactly in perfect harmony with nature, it was not in conflict with it either. The pink geyser existed in its own realm, alien yet legible. Part fantasy, part reality.

*

The geyser erupted again. The crowd applauded. Jean found herself dismayed it wasn't pink. I'm not sure what all the fuss is about, Annaliese said. Jean shrugged. It was too hard to be impressed by nature in wet socks and freezing rain. They posed for a few obligatory photos for friends back home and then left, anxious to be back on the road.

Hours later they arrived home soaked and cold, ready for sleep. But Jökull had other plans. First, he promised to make them a nice dinner, which they gladly accepted. This turned out to be spaghetti — not particularly exciting, but they were both too famished and exhausted to complain. Too late, they realised he thought of this as an exchange and expected something in return. He put on a French arthouse film about a threesome Jean had already seen, and shot them both hungry glances. When this didn't work, he tried to play them against each other. First one to give me a little kiss gets a spot in my bed, he said. She and Annaliese just looked at each other and laughed, then changed the subject. They were not going to trade spaghetti and a comfortable bed for sex. Jean thought Annaliese was beautiful and would've slept with her in a second, but she gave off very straight energy. After the film ended, Jean tried to announce that she was going to sleep. But Jökull forbade it, insisting that it was Friday night, they must all go out to the clubs. She reluctantly agreed, not wanting to be an impolite guest.

The three of them wandered the drag of perhaps five main clubs in Reykjavik. The only differences Jean could discern were that some of the clubs played techno, some played house, and some charged too much for drinks. Because it was summer, the midnight sun was out, giving everything a surreal touch. The silver light made for a grotesque spectacle, illuminating young people vomiting on the cobblestones, stripped of the secure cover of night.

Around 4 am, Jean announced she would return to the flat, assuming Annaliese would accompany her. Instead, she gave Jean an apologetic shrug. Jean felt betrayed, a sudden gulf forming between them. She already sensed what would happen in the morning, Annaliese silently emerging from Jökull's bedroom in only a slip. She walked back alone under the glaring sun, her feet blistered and sore.

When she returned, Jean collapsed on the pull-out couch. She dreamt about columns of water shattering in the air, sediment spilling over the tiles, searching for a way back to the sea.

*

Suddenly, it was her last day in Iceland, and she intended to spend it as far away from Jökull's flat as possible. She was hungover, and also somewhat depressed by her time in the city. She crawled into the darkest bar she could find and settled in to read. She was trying her best to nurse a beer when the man who would later become her husband walked in.

She was reading *Détruire, dit-elle* by Marguerite Duras, so he spoke to her in French, asking if she had seen the film by the same name. Jean was startled; first that someone would try and talk to her, and then that the man spoke French so well, when she could tell from his accent that he was Russian. Jean had always been a slut for accents. He sat down next to her and introduced himself as Konstantin, which sounded to her like a stampede of horses. He was a Russian-born poet currently living in London. He had just finished an artist residency in Reykjavik, and like her, the icy city drew a piercing loneliness out of him.

She found him extremely attractive, even without the accent. He had classic Eastern European features she liked; a prominent nose, thick eyebrows, and a fiery gaze. His hair was the colour of oak, falling over his eyes. Instead of feeding her lines, he shared that he loved to fish and to write poems about his grandfather, which she found endearing. After a few drinks, he turned to her and said softly:

Can I tell you something?

Eyes wide, she nodded.

I'm not really in Reykjavik for the residency. Well, not just that. A friend of mine died, a year ago today. I wanted to be as far away from home as possible.

He didn't meet her gaze, suddenly shy.

Oh, god, that makes sense. I'm so sorry.

Don't be. Yuri, my friend, he'd been . . . not well for some time. I apologise, I probably shouldn't have told you that.

No, not at all. I don't mind.

I just had a feeling that you are someone who can handle dark things.

Jean took this as a compliment. Konstantin, now eager to change the subject, unearthed a package of cigarettes.

Do you smoke?

She hadn't had a cigarette in days. Her body ached for nicotine. They smoked and flirted for hours, arguing about literature, art, film, philosophy, and language. He was thrilled to discover that she'd majored in Russian and French in college, and that she knew about the singer Vladimir Vystosky and the surrealist writer Daniil Kharms. They had switched to English but when Konstantin got passionate he would slip into Russian without realising.

Unlike Jean, he believed in absolutes; black and white, conviction. When she told him she was a translator, he responded by telling her all books were better in the original language. There was no comparison. It's not an art, he said firmly. Instead of feeling insulted, Jean was determined to convince him he was wrong. She pulled out her notebook and showed him some of her recent translations of poems by Anne-Marie Alonzo. As he read them over, he broke into a smile.

These are very good, he admitted. You're talented. Still, I guarantee they will never match the originals. They can't.

The point is not to match the original, she responded softly.

Untranslatability was the only area where they agreed; both were fans of Emily Apter. Certain ideas could not migrate from one language to another, there being a kind of violence in the attempt. Konstantin gave as an example une expression idiomatique: rire jaune. Literally, to laugh yellow. But meaning something more like laughing with pain, a forced smile, a nervous laugh. In this case, Jean would settle for a similar expression in translation, while Konstantin advocated taking it out of the manuscript altogether. He believed the most difficult terms to translate were philosophical ones like Heidegger's Dasein. Jean, who didn't give a fuck about Heidegger, strongly disagreed.

Humour is the absolute hardest thing to translate well, she said. You try it sometime.

She was three beers in, her mind fuzzing, inhibitions melting away. They gravitated closer together as the afternoon faded, until they were just barely touching.

Finally, she dared to look at her watch and told him that, sadly, she had a plane to catch that evening. But maybe they could exchange emails and continue their discussion? She wasn't ready for it to end. Konstantin shook his head and placed one hand on her thigh. You're thinking too small, he replied. His residency was over, and he was ready to leave Reykjavik. Originally, he'd planned to stay in Iceland for a few more days, but now he wanted to get on the road, he explained. Berlin next, maybe Budapest, Paris, Morocco. She should come.

The money? Money is no problem, he said simply. Jean a ri jaune. She had no idea what he meant; of course it was a problem, one of the biggest problems in her life. She thought about it constantly. But then he clarified: It would be my pleasure to pay for you. His hand moved a little higher up her thigh, and she stirred, remembering how long it had been since she'd had sex. Even longer since she'd had good sex. The more turned on she got, the harder words became.

I have a job lined up in New York, she managed to say. Her old coworker had gotten her a hostessing job at a French restaurant. Her plan was to live in Queens for a bit and sublet while she figured her shit out. She was supposed to start after her Iceland trip.

What kind of job?

Hostessing, she admitted.

He laughed. You can get a hostessing job any time. I'm talking about something bigger, a huge opportunity.

This is insane, you don't even know me.

She hated herself for trying to talk him out of this, but she wasn't in a trusting mood after Jökull's nonsense. *Suivre un étranger à Berlin ? Désastre.*

You're right, I don't know you, he admitted. But there's something about you, Jean. And I've never been one to turn down a good experiment.

Hmmm, so that's what this was, she thought. *An experiment.* His hand brushed the scalloped trim of her underwear.

She could hide it no longer. Desire awoke, roared.

*

While Jean's flight to New York was boarding, she lay in Konstantin's hotel bed, his head between her thighs. He whispered to her in Russian, and she responded in French, until they found the place where their languages met.

He was nothing like her other lovers, which fascinated her. They were both so aroused it didn't take much, weeks of sexual frustration melting under the covers. They fucked for hours, destroying her clothes.

When it was over, a morose quiet fell on them like the forest after a storm. Searching for something to fill the silence, Konstantin unearthed a bottle of Icelandic schnapps called Svarti dauði — Black Death.

He filled two glasses and proposed a toast to whatever was happening between them. Jean drank in the blackness, and they embraced, looking out the window at the darkening purple sea.

The next day, they were off to Berlin.

Faux Amis

The beginning of their relationship was a tipsy flush, falling in love with potential, all problems yet to be uncovered. They travelled like two newlyweds, unable to stop touching. Every room was a new opportunity for sex, a game to see how much they could get away with. She kept a list: the public washroom, Tiergarten, the U-Bahn late at night, the zoo, some quick gropes in line at the döner shop before she ordered a kebab to go.

They arrived in Berlin determined to have sex, drugs, and wild abandon, and they found it, the dark streets lined with others seeking the same. People wanting to do heroin like Christine F., to drink themselves to death in the fabulous outfits from *Bildnis einer Trinkerin*. They snorted coke in a bathroom, and then Konstantin fucked her from behind in a photo booth, and they giggled like teens, waiting for their low-fi porn to print. She knew she and Konstantin were one of thousands of couples that had fucked in the photo booths, each thinking they were original. But every time she looked at the resulting strip, she got goosebumps.

Jean understood implicitly that if Konstantin was a poet, he must have a private source of income. He didn't volunteer any information, but she assumed it was family money. Someone in his life must've struck it rich at some point, probably oil. Jean was afraid to press him, not wanting to pry or to seem ungrateful.

His money acted like an iron, smoothing out all the troubles in their new, shared life. He ordered room service all the time, something Jean had only seen in movies. If they were a few minutes late for a train, they would simply buy new tickets. The same if they missed a film screening because they were too busy fucking again. Even when she ran out of birth control pills, they fucked anyway because he was able to pay for emergency contraception, or if it came to it, an abortion. If she was bored, if she was tired, if she was hungry, if they had a fight — money solved everything.

You don't understand, she thought. His world was hardback spines, violins, vacations in the snowy mountains. Jean's mother made her eat cereal with water a few times when they couldn't afford milk and her paycheck wasn't coming for another week. When there was no money for braces, she was told to push on her teeth every day. People she grew up with drove drunk across the icy roads on purpose, just because they were so fucking bored, because their lives felt so hopeless.

But with every day that passed, she became more adjusted to his lifestyle. She forgot about her old life. The day when she was supposed to start hostessing came and went. She didn't contact the restaurant. A few friends from college texted her, asking what she was up to. She ignored them. She started to feel completely detached, fully invested in her time with Konstantin.

The thing that surprised her most was that Konstantin did not seem to believe his bourgeois lifestyle was in conflict with left-wing politics. He espoused anti-capitalist beliefs, but his wallet was bulging with signature credit cards. He reminded her of a man she had once met in college who called himself an anarchist but lived in a New York brownstone his parents had purchased for $2 million. She went to visit him once at this apartment. In the living room, there was a vintage motorcycle painted white. He gave her a shot from his imported espresso machine while she flipped through an art book on his coffee table, a collection of posters and anecdotes from May '68. *Sous les pavés, la plage.* She wondered if he'd ever read it.

But what seemed like a serious ethical dilemma to her, or at best hypocrisy, did not bother Konstantin in the slightest. Part of this was due to his generosity. However much money he had, he was always giving it away to others. He was a big tipper and gave money to whoever he met on the street. He was happy to be anywhere and to talk to anyone, equally content in a squat or a gala. He had friends all over Berlin that they kept running into, people who seemed genuinely overjoyed to see him after years apart. She couldn't get a read on him.

The first few nights they spent in a hotel near Alexanderplatz. But after a few days, he asked if she wouldn't mind staying with a friend of his. She agreed happily, curious about his acquaintances.

His friend turned out to be an artist named Safiye who lived in Neukölln. Safiye worked at a daycare to pay the bills and the rest of the time made giant sculptures. She served them rosehip tea with sugar cookies. As she drank the overly sweetened tea, Jean registered that Safiye was about her age and very pretty. She started to put everything together. When they were alone for a second, she asked Konstantin outright.

Did you come here to sleep with her?

He smirked in reply, clearly enjoying himself.

She's an old flame, if that's what you're asking. But now, of course, I met you. He looked directly at her as he spoke. Are you jealous?

Jean wasn't sure what to say. She was unsure if she could trust Konstantin, and he was not encouraging her to trust him. He did not say: I won't sleep with Safiye. He did not say: you and I are dating. But Jean wasn't going to give him the satisfaction of knowing how jealous she was. The uncoolest possible woman was a jealous woman. So she said:

No, thank you for telling me.

She was afraid she would dislike Safiye, but found it impossible. She was open-hearted and lovely, lending Jean a bike and taking her on a tour of city gardens and markets while Konstantin met up with more old friends. They picked sunflowers as big as her head and a mountain of vegetables for dinner, while Safiye asked her a stream of questions about being a translator.

We owe a great debt to translators, as a society, Safiye said. I grew up here, but so many of my friends and neighbours struggle because they only speak Turkish or Arabic. I have friends who work with Syrian refugees and translate government documents for free.

Yes, yes, Jean said. She'd done that same type of work in college but didn't elaborate. She didn't want to talk about translation. This was her chance to learn more about Konstantin, and she wasn't going to pass it up.

She asked Safiye how they met.

Oh, he had just published that chapbook, you know, the one with the deer skull on the cover, she said. Jean didn't know. She was ashamed to realise she hadn't read any of his poetry yet. But she took it as a good sign he wasn't forcing it down her throat.

He read in Russian, at this Eastern European bookstore that's gone now, Safiye continued, but it was right down the street. I'll show you later. A friend of mine was reading with him, he asked me to translate Konstantin's poems into German as a favour, and then he read those afterwards.

You speak Russian?

Not well, but I lived in Moscow for a bit visiting a friend there, so I know enough to get by. You speak Russian, too?

Well, I studied it in college, I was a double Russian and French major.

Can I ask — why Russian?

Jean tried to figure out how to summarise that choice, which seemed so complicated at the time.

I liked the writers, Lyudmila Petrushevskaya, Marina Tsvetaeva, Daniil Kharms. But really, I think I needed to immerse myself in a language that was completely different from my own. It gave me a way to escape the demands of English and French, to escape even their alphabets.

Safiye smiled with recognition. Then she guided the conversation back to Konstantin:

Anyway, I thought his poems were stunning — even more so in German. And then we all went out, and then . . .

She gave Jean an embarrassed smile. Jean nodded, to let her know it didn't bother her.

What about you two? Safiye asked. Are you together?

Jean didn't know what to say. They were, technically, together. It should hold great weight for someone to take her on a vacation. But Konstantin was impulsive. She sensed that he could move on at any time.

We're friends, she told Safiye.

*

Safiye made lahmacun, which they devoured with icy bottles of Radeberger picked up at a Späti on their way home. For dessert, she served a blackberry lavender tart and gave Jean the largest slice. Konstantin was in an inspired mood when he returned from his adventures, praising Safiye's cooking and trying to dance around the kitchen with Jean, one hand on the small of her back. Her jealousy dissipated, reassured they were just three friends enjoying each other's company. She could be mature, she told herself.

When they finished eating, Konstantin suggested they go to a bar. They took the U-Bahn to a place in Friedrichshain that Safiye liked so that they could watch the dying sun streak along the Spree like a comet. A golden-red glow coated the weeping willows along the edges of the river, drunk branches kissing the water. Jean reluctantly admitted to herself it was a romantic sight, but would not permit herself to be overcome by atmosphere.

Safiye seemed to have some sort of flirty relationship with the bartender, and they playfully shoved one another. She insisted on ordering for everyone and came back with far more beers than she ordered, plus some shots of kirschwasser on the house.

As they toasted and took the shots, Jean felt special, like she'd transcended the role of tourist. Becoming part of the scenery, blending in. She was adding something, whereas tourists merely took. But just then, Safiye asked her where she was from. Jean hesitated.

Well, I was born in Montreal, but I spent most of my life in the U.S.

Montreal! I've never been to Canada. I couldn't place your accent, but there is something a bit French about it, so that makes sense.

Yeah, I grew up speaking English. I wasn't allowed to speak French at home. My mother and stepfather thought it would make things harder for me. But then, of course, it was forbidden fruit, and I wanted to learn it more than anything. She added, perhaps a little defensively:

Did you know Kerouac is French-Canadian? He grew up in Massachusetts, but he spoke French with his family.

You're fucking with us, Konstantin said playfully.

No, no, look it up. Jean-Louis Lèbris de Kirouac, or Kèrouac. That was his birth name, I swear.

She'd expected him to take her word for it, but he searched it immediately on his phone and showed the first result to Safiye. Jean watched their expressions transform.

I'll be damned, he is. I didn't take you for a Beat. Or a French-Canadian, for that matter.

I suppose I'm more American than French-Canadian at this point. I mean, I mostly grew up in Cleveland. I just went back to Montreal for the summers.

You did? Konstantin looked at her with renewed interest. She realised they somehow had never talked about her childhood.

Yeah, it's a long story.

Jean stood up, feeling like she had said too much. She went to examine the jukebox, flicking past dated Europop compilations, David Hasselhoff CDs, and handmade mixes, looking for something to orient her. Eventually she selected a Grace Jones track, a song for the haunting blue dusk in an unfamiliar city. Jones' voice exuded mystery. *Tu cherches quoi, rencontrer la mort? Tu te prends pour qui? Toi aussi, tu détestes la vie?*

When she returned to the table, she noted that Konstantin had finished his beer and moved closer to Safiye. They were looking at something on Safiye's phone and whispering in German. She suddenly felt rude, as if she was intruding on someone else's date. Not necessarily because of the physical proximity, which she sensed was a result of Konstantin's drunkenness. No, it was the intimacy of their German that made her feel intrusive. A place she could not go. They knew she could not understand them, shutting her out completely. She patiently waited for them to return to English or Russian, but they continued, oblivious to her presence. When Safiye got up to go to the bathroom, Konstantin finally remembered her.

Sorry, got a bit carried away, he said sheepishly. Jean knew to act cool. There was nothing wrong with two people speaking a language she didn't. That was the state of the world, an experience many people lived every day.

I'm going for a walk, she said, and he nodded, distracted.

Outside, she felt awful. De- and re-jected. She considered ending the trip then, leaving Konstantin. She ducked into a Späti and picked up a pack of cigarettes. As she inhaled the first, her calm came back.

Exhausted but not knowing why, she sat down on a bench to smoke, letting the cool night wash over her. She spotted a red balloon in the sky, maybe off to find ninety-eight more. A black shadow darted out from under a bush and made its way across the pavement. At first, she thought: rat. But when she saw a second one, she realised they were wild rabbits. She watched their noses twitch, reading the air, alert for any flicker of danger.

The city's wild rabbit population flourished during the early stages of the Berlin Wall. Jean had seen a Polish documentary about it in college called *Rabbit à la Berlin*. Her recollection was hazy now, she couldn't remember why the title was in French. Were the rabbits in colour, or black and white? She thought the story went something like: when the wall was constructed, the meadow at Potsdamer Platz became a prison for the unsuspecting rabbits. Safe from natural predators but unable to move beyond the thin strip of grass. They fucked like mad, and their population soared within months. She remembered that at first the guards at the wall were curious about the rabbits, watching them on their long shifts. She thought she recalled a few of them even trying to train the rabbits. But eventually they began to shoot and poison them with pesticides. Like most good art, the documentary wasn't really about just one thing.

When Jean watched the wall tumble down at the end of the film, all she could think was: what a fucking waste. Humans possessed so much intelligence and skill, and they used it to construct giant barriers to keep out ideas, as if ideas were some tangible thing that could be killed.

The rabbits hopped a bit closer to her, and she wished she had something to feed them, although she knew you weren't supposed to. She held out her hand anyway, making soft noises in the back of her throat. *Toi aussi, tu détestes la vie?* she asked them. But she didn't hate life. She'd made it all the way to Berlin, something she'd never imagined possible in a million years. For the first time, fortune seemed to be smiling on her.

The rabbits ventured a little closer but stopped at some invisible line in the grass and then would go no further. They looked at each other. Moonlight caught their eyes, dyed their fur silver. Jean had managed to forget about Konstantin and Safiye entirely. She was grateful to be alone at that moment, to not share it with anyone.

Masculin// Féminin

The next day was Sunday, so Safiye took them to Mauerpark for the flea market. The park was bustling with locals and tourists, people selling souvenirs, old clothes, and fried food.

Jean stopped to inspect a cluster of yellowing books splayed out on a blanket. She decided on a cheap copy of Simone de Beauvoir's *The Woman Destroyed.* She'd read the stories before, and they were far from her favourite of de Beauvoir's. She wanted it because the reprint cover was gorgeous. A pink background with a pair of floating lips smothered in green lipstick, smoking a cigarette. For €3, she could own a little portable work of art and adore something just for the sake of its beauty. When Konstantin asked her why she bought it, she was embarrassed and didn't mention the cover. I'm trying to read more short stories, she said.

He bought her a pair of silver earrings in the shape of snakes. They had little green stones embedded in them that were supposed to be scales.

If you're going to have hair that short, you might as well wear earrings, he said. She put them on. She didn't usually wear earrings anymore, but she would wear these for a little while, to make him happy.

I was right, they look great with your hair, Konstantin said, claiming victory.

She liked that her short haircut showed off her long neck and made her look androgynous. People said she resembled Jean Seberg in *Saint Joan* but with crooked teeth. They would usually add, reassuringly, that they *liked* crooked teeth. But Jean wanted to look like Maria Falconetti in *La passion de Jeanne d'Arc*. People complained that Seberg's good looks were frivolous in this situation, distracting from the seriousness the role required. What Jean wanted above all, was to be taken seriously.

She'd had short hair her entire life. It was a utilitarian choice more than an aesthetic one; she saved a lot of money on haircare and salons. But she couldn't deny that it had become part of her identity. She had never grown out of her tomboy phase, or maybe there was more to it than that.

She'd always found it interesting that the French term for *tomboy* was *garçon manqué*, not a perfect equivalent. Rather than boyish girl, it means failed boy. Pretend boy, deficient boy. This reminded her of Judeo-Christian attitudes, that Eve was ultimately leftovers made from Adam. Women as himitations, sloppy translations of male originals.

But Jean actually preferred *garçon manqué*, because it more accurately captured how she felt. Never a tomboy but a counterfeit man. She didn't even want to be a man but still felt as though, at some point, she had failed at the task of becoming one.

She played the part of the gamine, maybe too much so. Imitating a man caused trouble. She remembered Patti Smith telling a story about running into Allen Ginsberg at a diner. He thought she was a young man, flirting with her and offering to buy her a sandwich. When he realised he'd made a mistake, he was deeply upset. Can I still have the sandwich? she dared to ask.

In French, everything has to agree in case, number, gender. Elles aimaient le cinéma. Elles: third person, plural, feminine. In the real world, everything has to agree in face, body, gender: soft face and makeup, curves, female. Everything has to agree. Or there will be problems. A man kissed Jean in a dark bar once, believing she was also a man. When he felt one of her breasts, he yelled and shoved her, hard.

Can I still have the sandwich?

To Jean, it made no difference. She didn't see herself as a girl or a boy. She was a pair of lips, floating in the night.

*

Reluctantly, Jean came to the conclusion that she could not win against Safiye. Whatever Konstantin liked about her was something completely different than what he liked about Jean, and she was not going to convince him otherwise. In a similar sense, she was never going to convince him that the way he acted around Safiye constituted cheating, since they weren't even in a relationship. She knew any criticism or questioning on her part would only push him further away, so she avoided broaching the subject.

Instead, for the remainder of their stay, she put her energy into getting to know Safiye better and becoming her friend. She hoped that if Safiye became familiar, she would eventually cease to be a threat. Safiye welcomed this change in her demeanour, but it didn't stop her from continuing to flirt with Konstantin.

You'll never get him to settle down, Jean remembered her saying. I've known him for years. I don't care who you are. He's not that type of guy.

Even though she wasn't ever sure that they were actually friends, Jean believed Safiye. Konstantin wasn't that type of guy. OK, fine, but then what type of guy was he? Safiye didn't elaborate further. Jean knew then that she was in trouble. She was growing very attached to the poet. More than she wanted to acknowledge.

In those early days, Jean was very careful with everything she said and did around Konstantin. She feared that at any moment he would lose interest and see her not as cosmopolitan, but what she was: a woman with bad teeth, constructing a false self out of old books and films she'd consumed.

Francophony

They left Berlin after another week, for no particular reason that Jean could tell, besides that Konstantin was forever eager for the next new thing. They'd miss out on upcoming parties and shows. There was always something going on in Berlin that you'd be missing, but Konstantin thought that was ideal, to leave a place still wanting more. Better to depart before you get too comfortable, before you get bored, he said.

Jean, who was more than happy to leave Safiye behind, acquiesced to his wishes. He wouldn't tell her where they were going next, and by the time they got to the airport, it was too late for her to back out. She closed her eyes and tried to sleep the whole flight, until Konstantin's voice startled her awake.

Bienvenue à Paris, he said. As he smiled, she winced. For the first time, Jean found him tacky. She expected him to burst into song any minute now. He wanted to live in a Françoise Sagan novel, but she saw through the façade. At heart, Paris was just a city, a place like any other, intensely invested in reinforcing its own mythology.

Grinning, he said: You're going to love it.

Her burgeoning sense of dread deepened.

*

The truth was, in Paris, she felt like a fraud.

Her whole life, she'd absorbed the impression that the French-de-France were the real keepers of the language, while all other francophones were a poor imitation. She'd wanted to visit Paris since she was a little girl — everyone said it was a place for artists, rebels, romantics. But now that she was here, she only wanted to leave.

She'd been told outright before by people from France that Québécois French wasn't correct French but rather some unwanted bastard child. She found herself perpetually apologising: *Pardonnez-moi, pardon my French! Peut-être que si je travaille assez dur, un jour je serai capable de parler ma langue.* Her mother, Marie-Georges, had always been sensitive when French people gave up listening to what she said because they found her accent too difficult to understand. They nodded and smiled but wrote her off immediately; she spoke a bootleg language and needed to save up for name-brand French if she wanted to be treated better.

Paris. Jean was drowning in a sea of Audrey Tautou lookalikes who spoke Le Petit Robert French and rode bicycles with little baskets in the front. Fall looked good on Paris, red and orange leaves littering the ground, a light breeze stirring them to life every now and then. She watched the children leaving as schools let out, their careful outfits, tiny designer backpacks. Insecurity set in almost immediately. A Francophony. She feared everyone could read the inadequacy in her eyes. Every time Konstantin used the word *authentic* to describe something, she looked at the ground in shame. She would never have the Parisian girls' cool apathy towards others' opinions. Jean could not *not* care. She was not poised or confident enough to disregard the public, to not try to be liked.

She and Konstantin went to a café, listening carefully for other young bohemians, waiting for a moment to insert themselves. They sweated in the sun and drank bottle after bottle of Pschitt!, the soda's sound echoing its name every time they twisted off the top. Their desire to belong was embarrassing to Jean. They walked around Shakespeare and Company, loudly naming their favourite authors. When no one approached them, they gave up and talked to each other instead.

In Paris, Konstantin came out of his shell. He relaxed more and started to trust Jean enough to open up to her about his dead best friend. He spoke with great discomfort. His eyes welled up a few times, though he quickly brushed it away. She could tell he'd held this inside for ages and was dying to tell someone.

Yuri was from Saint Petersburg, where Konstantin was born. He was especially sensitive as a teenager — that was how Konstantin put it. He took in too much of the world. They'd stayed in touch and visited each other a few times over the years. Konstantin had tried to convince his friend to come join him in London, but he was too depressed.

I didn't understand, really, how quickly he was fading from everyone. I was too far removed. If I'd known, I would've gone to visit him sooner.

You couldn't have known though.

I should have. I feel so guilty. I was his best friend. His parents died . . . Really, when you got down to it, I was all he had. And now he's gone. I never went to a funeral, never saw a coffin . . . It was like he just vanished.

Jean nodded solemnly.

I'm sorry. I don't know what that was like, but I do know what it's like to lose people who are close to you.

She reached out and took his hand in hers.

Hearing about his love for Yuri moved her. She noticed that his demeanour was different and more open when talking about someone he cared for. When he dropped his mask of intellect, she really liked the man underneath. In fact, this made her like Konstantin perhaps more than anything else. Of course, it wasn't that she wished for people to suffer, but she found it difficult to relate to people who had never experienced suffering. There was wisdom that came with being dealt a bad hand in life. And although he had grown up with many material comforts she had not, Konstantin did know about real loss.

*

As the days passed, Jean realised that Konstantin was in search of a different Paris than her, something stunning, something black and white, like a shot from *Love on the Left Bank*. Jean saw herself as the protagonist of a film (or at the very least a major character), with Paris as the backdrop, while Konstantin saw Paris as the protagonist of their story. Il voulait Paris avec un passé exsangue. His only exception to this was the struggles of French revolutionaries. He wanted something to worship uncritically, and nothing, nothing was going to spoil it. This came to a head as they were strolling along the Seine, planning out the rest of their day. They'd been walking around since 8am on nothing but coffee, and Jean was starting to get extremely hungry. Konstantin went off on a long tangent about *Les Misérables* and Javert. He argued that Javert redeemed himself through his poetic suicide. The words *poetic suicide* made Jean physically sick. She looked out at the steel-grey water, unable to meet his eyes.

The river's very pretty.

You seem sad.

I'm not.

Well, you're definitely thinking about something.

No, no, it's nothing.

He didn't say it, but she could tell Konstantin was already disappointed that she wasn't as excited about Paris as him. She wanted to make his ego feel better. So she forced a smile, and they walked into a nearby pâtisserie to share some madeleines. There was a line snaking outside, large glass windows and overhead lights showcasing the rows of pastries like featured pieces in a gallery. Jean remembered something. In college her class was discussing Proust's madeleine and a woman, an American, probably Southern, came in late and pronounced it Prow-st. The professor swiftly corrected her over the soft current of snickering. The look on her face. She remembered how she too harshly judged this young woman, suddenly seeing her in a different light; foolish, her wool skirt appearing more pathetic than before.

But then Jean immediately admonished herself — after all, what did it matter? Had she herself never pronounced a word wrong? Had she not, just a month or two ago, murdered the spelling of baba ganoush on her grocery list? And what did wrong mean, anyway?

Sure, some agreement was necessary for communication, but these slight nuances, saying Prowst instead of Proust, why did this mean she was less intelligent? People liked to think themselves better than others because of spelling, grammar, punctuation, all these make-believe requirements they'd crafted to maintain a hierarchy of social classes. Without the shield of these rules, she knew, they were all the same.

As they waited in line at the pâtisserie, Serge Gainsbourg's voice drifted from a CD player. Everything around them screamed FRANCE! They were in FRANCE! And FRANCE! was a solid thing, a white marble statue, a silk scarf but never a headscarf, a painting you could admire from afar, even approach a little, but not get too close to without setting off security alarms.

She thought of an experimental film she'd seen in college, *Perfumed Nightmare*, by Kidlat Tahimik. The main character arrives in Paris from the Philippines shouting the four pillars of the West: "'Liberté, Egalité, Fraternité, Supermarché!'" Maybe Konstantin liked to think he was better than that, but really, what was the difference between the pastries and bohemian books he purchased and an Eiffel Tower figurine with a made-in-China sticker on the bottom? Didn't they serve essentially the same purpose?

Jean felt like it was impossible to have a single experience in Paris that was new, to think of a single original thought that someone else had not had before. All around her were people using the city as a vehicle for personal transformation. L'idée de Paris était si grande que la ville s'effondrait sous le poid. La ville de lumière, la ville de l'amour, la capitale de la mode, Lutèce, Paname, toutes ses personnalités et incarnations. Paris faisait des promesses qu'elle ne pouvait pas tenir.

She asked Konstantin why French people whispered in songs.

It's unnerving, she added. He shrugged.

You're more French than I am. I ought to be asking you that. I think it's supposed to be sexy? Pillow talk.

She shook her head as the answer dawned on her:

It's because they're hiding something.

*

Jean's greatest fear was that Konstantin would never want to leave Paris. Qu'il s'attarde, absorbant ce que les Français possédaient qu'elle manquait. The more enamoured he grew with Paris, the more he praised it, the more she tried to impress him. She found herself competing for his attention again, just as she had with Safiye. She scoured discount stores for new, flashy clothes, ones that didn't suit her. She knew this wasn't healthy; this wasn't the first time she'd tried to convince someone to like her.

In the end, she couldn't keep it up. The act got to be too much. While he went off on adventures, she feigned illness and hid in their hotel, depressed, reading books she'd bought and trying not to feel ashamed. In those moments, she longed for Montréal, for the bookstores and silver maple trees and dépanneurs selling cartons of tiny strawberries and familiar streets and the comforting presence of Mont. Royal, her silent guardian. Montréal felt knowable and real while Paris was disorienting, enigmatic.

She took refuge on the balcony of their hotel, chain-smoking Gauloises and re-reading *The Woman Destroyed*, watching the street below in between chapters. But she wasn't even managing that correctly; she thought of Leslie Caron in *An American in Paris* dressed exquisitely in black against a gold background, doing her ballet stretches without pausing her reading. Eyes glued to her book as she contorted her body into different shapes. Gracieuse et élégante. Jean feared she was neither.

She decided to take her book on a field trip to the cemetery Père Lachaise, which as a private joke she always called Father Thechair. The cemetery was busy even in the early morning, tourists heading straight for Oscar Wilde, Edith Piaf, Jim Morrison. She lost herself amongst the blue-green oxidised statues, rows of mausoleums displaying wealth inequality even in death, the fresh flowers and wreaths showing who was cared about, who had won.

She knelt in front of an unmarked grave, neglected and overgrown with moss, dipping her hands in the soil, coming up with dirt under her fingernails. She could hear sparrows chirping in the background. The air was so peaceful.

Inside, she was experiencing a metamorphosis. Still Jean, but here she was a leaner, more masculine Jean. La fille de Jean Genet. She thought of Genet now, although he was not buried at the cemetery. Genet died at Jack's Hotel in the 13th arrondissement. You could rent the room where they found his corpse for €95 a night or slightly more for a breakfast buffet included. She thought about all the dead, queer French men she loved: Jean, Hervé, Muzil. Elle imagine leurs fantômes hantant les coins oubliés. Hervé snapping photos and writing about Vincent in his notebooks; Muzil checking his citations at the library; then the two meeting for a walk, perhaps to gossip a little. Baldwin's spectre, drinking coffee at Le Select and scrawling notes to himself. It wasn't all bullshit.

After paying her respects at Père Lachaise, she went to a nearby bookstore and was pleased to see they had a selection of Dany Laferrière titles. She got to talking with a woman who owned the store, introducing herself as a literary translator. The woman was dressed rather intentionally, a black velvet ribbon tied around her blonde hair like something out of *Les*

Parapluies de Cherbourg. Eventually, salivating as though she had been waiting for the entirety of their conversation to ask, the woman said, smiling:

Vous avez un accent si curieux, je ne peux pas le dire. D'où venez-vous?

Jean instinctively crossed her arms around her chest in protection. She'd been found out. She tried so hard to adopt a neutral accent. But there was no such thing. She wanted to say something confusing, something that would make the woman feel guilty. But she knew what the woman meant: her French did not pass for French. After beginning the conversation in French, she'd quickly switched to English, which felt like an indictment.

Montréal.

This statement felt to her half truth and half lie.

Oh! The woman clapped her hands together, as though overcome with joy. This seemed like a performance to Jean. It was meant to make her feel better, when it only did the opposite.

I've never been, but my cousin owns an apartment there. She splits her time; rents it out half the year on Airbnb then spends the rest of her time in Nice. Anyway, I love your accent! It's so... rustic, so, how do you say... chantant. Singing. Sways as you speak.

Mm.

This was the most Jean could bring herself to say through tight lips. It wasn't fair, that was the short of it. She didn't even have a Québécois accent, anyone who lived there would tell her as much. All the woman heard was difference, that she stuck out. There was nothing she could say to mock this woman's accent in return. She could not offend her, because her culture was popular. The woman did not even understand that she was being offensive, that was the worst part. She was slapping her, over and over, and not understanding why Jean's face got so red.

My cousin, she says the Québécois speak terrible French, but that can't be true, look at you! Of course not, I know education was bad in your country for a long time though. So people must be catching up.

Years later when she recalled this moment, it would still burn just as freshly. Every time she felt insecure, she would remember the attractive woman in the bookstore who said such ugly things. Jean imagined how much worse it might have been were she Black. She thought of Fanon's *Peau noire, masques blancs* that she'd read in her college classes, and how the more that Antilleans could demonstrate their ability to speak "proper" French, the more they were seen as human. Jean often had her French abilities questioned, but never her humanity.

More sentences were coming out of the woman's mouth, but Jean had stopped listening. She could see the words now, disassociated from the woman's body, black letters like cut up newspaper headlines floating in the air between them, arranging and rearranging themselves. She watched them float, amused. They were toothless now, like styrofoam in a snow globe. They could transform into any word, any sentence. These letters did not belong to this woman whose name she didn't even know. There was a reason they called them characters, entities with their own autonomy.

She reached out to touch one, a svelte lowercase *j*. The letter evaded her touch, slipping away just as she tried to grab it. She was no longer aware of the woman's presence or of anyone else in the bookstore.

Resignification, she murmured aloud, which at the time felt like a very astute observation.

The woman squinted and looked at her in confusion.

Yes, resignification. What do you mean by that?

Oh, nothing. I'm not sure you would understand, Jean replied.

She left the store without further explanation, a stolen copy of *Mille plateaux* tucked under her coat.

Rose Sauvage

To Jean's great relief, within a week, Konstantin's obsession with Paris soured. He was not finding enough of what he'd pined for, the city failing to live up to his dreams. The experience he was seeking, he complained, was long gone.

By this point, she was starting to feel very guilty. This was the longest she'd ever gone without working in her life. She was supposed to be in New York. She was letting people down. But she also had to admit she wasn't ready to leave Europe yet. She refused to connect to Wi-Fi. No messages came in, she could ignore the real world a little longer.

Konstantin got into their rental car, grinning. Their next destination, he promised, would be a surprise. *NO, please* she thought, *no more surprises.* She said nothing.

She became increasingly panicked as they left Paris behind. Dug her nails into her palm, kept changing the radio station. Maybe he was finally leaving her for Safiye. Maybe he wanted a threesome. Maybe he would humiliate her, tell her he had finally come to his senses and leave her by the side of the road.

Instead, he drove them straight into a mirage, a living Impressionist painting. Feral white horses with grey muzzles running through the marsh, traditional steeds of the gardians. Jean had never seen wild horses and rarely even seen domesticated ones except at the zoo or on television. A new type of wonder arose within her, the wonder she'd wanted to feel in Iceland. Awe, she realised. Magnificent, galloping awe.

Once they spotted a herd, Konstantin stopped the car and cut the engine. For the most part the horses ignored them and continued to graze, indifferent to human presence. They knew they were in no danger of being tamed. When she and Konstantin had their fill, they drove on, looking for more horses hidden in the reeds, climbing down the narrow wooden boardwalks to stare in amazement at the salt flats.

But the real stars of the show were the flocks of wild flamingos in the palest baby-pink she had ever seen. Some so lightly coloured they looked like ghosts. Breathlessly, she watched them, legs mired like thin stilts in the brine ponds, delicate feathers fluttering in the breeze. Fragile, as though they might blow away at any moment.

You like it? Konstantin asked.

She nodded emphatically, no words enough to express the feeling in her chest. She loved it, and she loved him for sharing it with her. She struggled to believe any of it could be real. Another dimension assembled from dreams. She wanted to find a way to keep it, to bottle the strange place and return to it in her mind. When they stopped at a little roadside store, she bought a large bottle of water and a postcard of La Camargue, knowing even then that she would never send it. A thin slice of cardboard, cut into quarters with four different shots. White horses *flash!* then flamingoes with black-tipped wings in flight *flash!* black bulls *flash!* then a lone gardian wandering through the reeds. As if she had not purchased an object but her own memory. Their trip so neatly matched up with the photos, except the very last one, like a skipped beat.

She wanted to make that surreal day with Konstantin into something material she could hold onto, something that wouldn't be lost to time.

(Ex)hibition

A single black stiletto heel, backlit.
The crust from a scab, resting in a Petri dish.
A ceramic heart with red and blue glass beads inside.
A chipped garden gnome, most of its face missing.
An engraved pocket knife from WWII.
A broken ceramic vase with flowers on the sides.

These were some of the exhibits on display at the Muzej prekinutih veza, or the Museum of Broken Relationships in Zagreb, the last stop on their trip. Konstantin wanted to go somewhere new, somewhere different, that neither of them had ever been before. Jean could choose where, he offered, it would be his pleasure. Her suggestion of Croatia came as a surprise, she couldn't explain why, she was just drawn to it.

That was how they ended up at the museum, an impulse decision based on a brochure found in a café. Each object in the exhibit was accompanied by a short plaque in English and Croatian. There were a range of stories, from humorous to devastating. Cheating was a frequent subject. The majority of the items were from romantic relationships, but for Jean some of the most upsetting were the ones from children abandoned by their parents, wounds that lasted a lifetime.

She paused in front of a dark blue vase broken into neat, large pieces. White enamel flowers adorned some of the shards. Whoever had brought the vase in appeared to have taken great care to collect all the individual pieces. Had the vase fallen? Or had someone smashed it in anger? The enigmatic plaque revealed nothing. *You were the one who broke the vase, I was always the one who tried to put it back together*, read the script.

The longer Jean stared, the more she drank in the heavy atmosphere, until she started to choke on the psychic weight of human heartbreak and misery. She thought of her parents, of what might have been. The museum was a sobering reminder that the majority of relationships disintegrated, that sustained human connection was still one of the hardest things to achieve in any culture. The objects started to overwhelm Jean until she was anxious to go. She couldn't shake the eerie feeling she had been here before, maybe in a dream. She nudged Konstantin, but he was still reading the plaques, deep in thought.

What are you thinking? She asked, suddenly needy, eager for his attention. For whatever time they had left together.

He shrugged. She could tell he wasn't as troubled by the museum as she was. Finally he elaborated:

It's certainly an interesting exercise, to try and narrate the whole story of a relationship based on a single item. He smiled like he was picturing a particular item, a particular relationship.

She shook her head.

These people are haunted. I think probably this kind of thing helps with healing, moving on.

Maybe they should be haunted. I mean, just passing on your baggage to a museum isn't really dealing with it, is it? It's a reification, almost. Putting it on display.

She couldn't help but feel that his remarks were pointed.

No, no. I don't think they're coming back here to look at the objects. I think it's the same as giving them away to a charity. And maybe as a lesson for others, to avoid future breakups?

That's a bit optimistic. Breakups are as old as time itself. They're not going to stop anytime soon.

She didn't like the way their conversation was going. Jean left him to study the exhibits while she browsed the gift shop, picking over the limited edition, small-run art prints she could not afford. The two of them were so recent, so undefined, that it felt absurd to imagine the end of their story, to talk about their relationship in the past tense. She suspected it was coming, though. She was aware that they would not be isolated, youthful, and on vacation for the rest of their lives. And she feared that, without those very specific conditions, they would get along as well as they did.

But Jean was a romantic. She would have liked to freeze both of them in the museum as artefacts. Two wasps trapped side by side in a thick golden tomb of amber. Forever, happy.

III. Safe European Home

The trip was ending, and the future of their relationship was like the bottom of a lake to Jean — confusing, murky. Whenever she tried to bring this up, Konstantin assured her that they'd figure it out but never said anything specific beyond that. She'd decided she did not want to return to Canada or the United States. Legally, though, she needed a job or another reason to stay in Europe for an extended period of time.

They ended up back at his flat in Soho. After all their weeks abroad, Konstantin finally seemed eager to return to familiarity, and Jean didn't object. He opened the door to his place, ordering any burglars to vacate with a laugh. Jean stared openly. His place was a reflection of him, or the version of himself he wanted to project to the world — minimal, neat, well kept. There were a few framed photos on the walls of his family and one of him standing next to a serious young man with a shaved head she assumed was Yuri. The bookcases were stocked with gilded hardbacks Jean had never seen anywhere. Coffee table books of elegant erotic photos in black and white, rare tomes from the 1800s, first editions of poetry. She marvelled once again at her luck running into Konstantin in Iceland, of all places. Presque destiné.

If they'd stayed together in his flat right away that first month, Jean had a feeling they might never have become a serious couple. Reality would've kicked in, and they would've grown to annoy one another in the tight quarters. But Konstantin was one step ahead of this. In a stroke of genius, without so much as a note or a phone call, he left her there. She woke up in his bed alone, bewildered and a little scared.

The result was that her feelings for him, so tangled up in their travels, had time to deepen and crystallise. He'd only been gone a few hours, but she missed him more than she'd imagined possible. And she'd never missed a lover before. People came and went from her life, and she never objected. One lover gone left space for another to enter. After her father left, Jean had trained herself not to get too attached to people. She believed nothing was permanent, even love. And yet she couldn't get Konstantin out of her mind. She wondered what he was doing, was he thinking of her, too. Was he at work? What did going to work mean for a poet, anyway, visiting a café? Had something terrible happened to him? When would he come back?

The longing made her feel juvenile and weak. She had no appetite. He'd left a key on the kitchen table, and she tried it in the lock. It worked; she could leave the flat if she wanted. But she remained stupidly stuck in his kitchen. She started chain smoking out the window, turning into a little wisp of smoke. Sucking in the new London air and polluting it with herself, her nicotine, until they matched.

Then, it occurred to her that she did know one person besides Konstantin in London. Relieved, she immediately messaged her friend on WhatsApp, checking every few minutes for a reply. Nat messaged back shortly to say that they were busy but could meet for a drink the next day. Jean agreed, pleased to have plans.

Nat picked a nondescript pub for their meet-up, the type with a lion or swan on the sign, where the air smelled of expired yeast and grizzled men eyed you suspiciously. Jean was almost twenty minutes late but relaxed once she spotted a tall, androgynous person walking in wearing a shirt that said: *I'm not straight, but £20 is £20.* That had to be Nat.

The trick, she thought, if you were the kind of person who was constantly late, was to have friends who were equally or even more late, so that no one was upset and waiting alone. Nat was Jean's friend in college but they moved to London for work shortly after. Jean didn't keep up with most people from college. When she left a place, she generally cut all ties, leaving the people and her feelings about them behind as well. But Nat had made a real effort to stay in touch with her, and Jean reciprocated. As with most of Jean's friends, their history was a little complicated.

Jean immediately took note of the ruggedly handsome queer sitting in the back of her Russian class, hair slicked back and feet propped on the desk like they were in a movie. At the time, Jean was majoring in Russian and French, working her hardest to improve at both languages. Nat was the product of a Russian mother and a Hungarian father, both Canadian immigrants. Exceptionally lazy, they were majoring in Russian, pretending they were not a native speaker because it was an easy pass. Jean remembered when she caught Nat talking on the phone to their grandmother in perfect Russian, how instead of annoying she just found it funny, impressive. Jean doubted she'd ever see Nat again after their class was over, but they ended up at several queer dance nights together, sharing coke and ecstasy. Still, it took weeks before they had a real conversation. Jean found Nat attractive and often got tongue-tied talking to attractive people. So she was grateful when Nat initiated, and they ended up having sex in the bathroom at a party, even though Nat had a girlfriend at the time. This wasn't a big deal to Jean, who slept with everyone in college. Her speciality was unavailable types — married men, women still in love with someone else, her professors.

College was the first time Jean ever remembered consciously shifting her identity. She became someone new every time she had a one-night stand; she'd never see them again, so what did it matter who she was? Shapeshifting was a skill she picked up from her short stint working for a phone sex hotline. As soon as someone called in, she'd give a description of the character she'd invented for the job: Joanie. Joanie was petite yet busty and blond with a soft voice. And the man would say, Oh, that's too bad, I'm into statuesque brunettes with giant asses. In her naïvetè, Jean assumed she'd simply transfer the man's call to another woman working at the hotline whose character fit the bill. But what she was actually instructed to do was simply *tell* the man she was transferring him and then re-answer the phone herself in a different voice, claiming to be Jana, a sultry, tall brunette. She could never tell if the men bought it or if they accepted the façade as part of the game. She was best at her job when she could fully immerse herself into the new role and believe for those few minutes, until the man climaxed, that she was Jana and Jana was her.

Sometimes the men wanted something else. Jean was only willing to take it so far. If they asked for a Black or Indigenous woman (they did not use those words), she'd pretend the call dropped and swiftly hang up. After this happened a few times, her boss found out and fired her.

She never worked for a hotline again, but that ability to slip into someone else's life, their mind, stayed with her. She found it intoxicating. Sometimes she did it without even realising. Later, she found this same feeling through translation.

Nat knew her as Jeanne, a young woman rediscovering her French-Canadian heritage. So they were surprised to hear that she was going by Jean now.

What prompted the change? Was it a gender thing? A quarter-life crisis thing? An American thing? Was she trying to distinguish herself from her parents? Je ne sais pas, she shrugged. She was just someone else. Sitting across from each other over their glasses of lager, both sensed the sexual tension still lingering between them. Things were different now though, and they both did their best to prove to the other how adult they were. Nat, for their part, had a job at an LGBTQ youth centre, several bizarre cats, and a partner named Jody who was a sex therapist.

So, Nat said, taking a sip of their beer. A foam of moustache on their upper lip. What have you been up to? We all expected great things of you.

Jean told them about her travels, Iceland and all the rest, spending the most time on her descriptions of the flamingos. Only at the end did she mention she'd been with Konstantin the whole time.

Ohhhh interesting. There's a man.

Yeah. I don't know if it's serious.

Jean wasn't sure why she said this, when she wanted it to be serious. Maybe to protect herself.

Cool, cool. But you're staying with him?

For now, yes.

Jean felt embarrassed. Nat said everyone expected big things of her, but what had she done since college? Gone on vacation with her boyfriend. Maybe not even her boyfriend. Just then, as if Konstantin could read her mind, her phone buzzed. The first time he'd made contact with her since he left.

The text was a photo of a statue, a woman with a sword kneeling in prayer.

Emilija Pliateryte

he wrote.

> She's like the Lithuanian
> or Polish Joan or Arc,
> she fought against us
> in the November Uprising.
> Reminds me of you.

So he was either in Lithuania or Poland, she hadn't expected either of those. Jean was amused by the comparison to Emilija. She wasn't really sure any part of her reminded Konstantin of the revolutionary countess. But she appreciated the subtext: he was thinking of her. She wanted to message him back but stopped herself; he needed to think she was busy, that she had other things to occupy her thoughts besides him. She grinned and put the phone away.

You look so happy! Was that him? Nat asked. Jean nodded, blushing.

I'm sorry, that was rude of me.

No, no it's fine. It was so great to hear from you, Jean. Do you know how long you're staying?

Not really. I haven't figured anything out yet.

Well, even if you're only in town for a little while, you should come to karaoke tonight, meet Jody and my friend Layla. I think you'd really get along.

Hmmm, okay. Karaoke is really not my kind of thing.

But Nat was already smiling their most convincing smile, the kind that always got Jean to break into pools and to skinny dip in college.

Yeah, yeah, all right. I'll come.

Perfect. It's not too far from here, we can take the Tube. Damn. I'm so glad you're here! I honestly never thought I'd see you again.

Yeah, Jean admitted. That's kind of my thing; I disappear.

But Nat just smiled. They didn't seem too concerned.

Well, let's see if we can't get you to stick around London for a bit.

They finished their beers and headed off to karaoke.

*

Jean was not used to missing people, but Konstantin was different. It unnerved her that he'd managed to get under her skin, somewhere close to her core. He wrote her emails signed "Yours," and she tried not to overinterpret this gesture. But she wanted to be his.

Being with him all day every day for so long, and then suddenly cut off completely, created a fierce longing in her similar to withdrawal.

Her feelings weren't just about Konstantin though. To her surprise, Jean liked being anchored. For years, she'd avoided getting into serious relationships because she didn't want any restraints. But now, thousands of miles away from home, the prospect of partnership was no longer frightening. A week after he'd left, she lay stretched out like a cat on his sofa, leafing through a pile of his books and considered that perhaps she just had never met anyone she could consider an equal. Peut-être qu'elle pourrait rester avec cette personne, cet endroit, pendant un certain temps. Peut-être que ce n'était pas une faiblesse de s'attacher à quelqu'un. Elle rêvait des choses qu'ils pourraient accomplir ensemble, de la vie merveilleuse qu'ils pourraient bâtir à deux.

And so, by the time Konstantin returned from a week-and-a-half trip that he eventually explained was to Poland, Lithuania, and Belarus, she was his. She would've done anything to stay in his cosy apartment, sit on his lap of luxury, and drink tea, his reassuring arm curved around her waist. She fit into his life so easily. He'd missed her too, he told her. He'd brought her little trinkets — a ceramic mug, a bar of chocolate, three nesting dolls that looked up at her expectantly with wide eyes. This was the irrefutable proof she'd been looking for that she was in his thoughts.

The week after he got back, he was giving a reading in Russian at the kind of trendy new bar that served everything with paper straws that disintegrated immediately upon usage, near Covent Garden. He apologised and promised that the reading would be unforgivably dull, but she was welcome to show up. She did, surprised at how packed the place was for mostly unknown poets, until she realised people were there for the free wine and cheese. A few of the people there were Konstantin's friends, and like Safiye, they tended to be mostly young, highly intelligent, and beautiful.

Hoping to avoid her jealousy altogether, she struck up a conversation in French after the reading with an older man from Vendée. He reminded Jean a lot of her grandfather, salt-and-pepper hair and a fisherman's cap, but when he opened his mouth the similarities stopped. It took her only a few minutes to realise he was extremely conservative and anti-immigrant, and the conversation took a sharp turn, but she refused to back down. He began to rail against écriture inclusive and gender-neutral writing, the kids these days and their ridiculous, made-up pronouns.

Alors, tous les mots sont fabriqués. C'est le but du langage, she said with a shrug.

Vous me comprenez. Les mots officiels, du dictionnaire.

Le dictionnaire souligne l'usage populaire des mots, et non l'inverse.

The man's wrinkled face reddened, and he clutched his wine glass a little too tightly. He took the opportunity to pivot and instead insult her French, telling her of course she wouldn't understand, clearly English was her first language. She replied that she was French-Canadian, and he laughed nastily, saying that was even worse. She winced, remembering the woman at the bookstore in Paris. Just then, Konstantin appeared by her side.

What's that? he asked the man. The man looked confused for a second, but then he recognised Konstantin as one of the poets who had just read.

This young lady was trying to tell me about my language, and I was correcting her. She does not understand enough about this to have an opinion.

Konstantin gave Jean a look.

Is that so?

Well, you're Russian, I'm sure it's different. But French-Canadians, we do not see their language as *our* French, vous comprenez. They don't have the same conventions, the same rules. I don't mean any offence, but it's not what we would consider proper French.

Jean's face got hot. She was about to respond when Konstantin jumped in.

Listen, sir, all due respect — if you are so protective of language and against linguistic diversity, I'm not sure why the hell you came to a poetry reading in the first place. For instance, within different strands of Russian we have vowel reduction or lack thereof —

akanye or okanye. One is not more correct than the other. Language has always changed, which is why you do not currently speak Old French or Vulgar Latin. The way we pronounce a word today may not be the way we pronounce it in fifty years. Poetry, in my opinion, embraces this fluidity. And let me tell you, Jean speaks and writes excellent French. She knows and cares more about languages than anyone I've ever met, so don't you dare tell me she can't have an opinion about her own fucking language.

Jean was smiling so hard her face hurt. She admired the way he spoke about her, the way he picked up on the exact things she wanted people to see. The man, flustered, muttered curses under his breath at both of them, then excused himself. Konstantin shrugged and turned to her.

Wanker.

Yeah, thank you for saying something.

Of course. I know you're more than capable of defending yourself, but he just made me so angry, I couldn't help it.

If she thought about it from a certain angle, there was something condescending about his running to her defence, but in the moment she was relieved. She'd been too emotional right then to make all the points that needed to be made.

No, no. I'm glad.

And she was. Before, Jean was never sure where she stood with Konstantin, what she meant. But that night, his gesture demonstrated to her that he was someone who had her back, who understood what she was about, and who would stand up for her when it mattered.

*

One night, a couple of weeks later, they were watching *Eurovision* together. She'd never heard of it before. He patiently explained all the intricate politics behind the scenes, the way countries voted together in blocs with neighbouring ones. There was very real resentment simmering behind the glittering costumes, synths, and coloured light displays.

During a commercial break, Konstantin stood up. His face pale, strained in concentration.

I have something to tell you, he said. Jean held her breath, terrified of what he might confess about his time away, who he might have been with. She looked up at him.

Я тебя люблю, he said.

Grinning from ear to ear, she said that she loved him, too.

*

Jean adored her first months in London, the frenetic energy buzzing everywhere. It was exactly what the movies had told her it would be like. There was always somewhere to go, something to do, someone to be. Most of the museums were free. The parks were so lush, her favourite place to read. She hung out with Nat and her other new friends almost every week, grateful to have met people who already knew the best bars and clubs, a shortcut to the heart of the city. Nat was right; she loved karaoke and she loved Jody and Layla who were sharp and brutally funny. London was such a big place that she sometimes got overwhelmed, but her smaller world within it — her friends and Konstantin — made it feel manageable.

Close to half a year passed by quickly, until suddenly, Jean had to either get a job or she would be kicked out of the country. A panic came over her. She wasn't ready to leave, and she had nothing, absolutely nothing, to go back to. Even so, she considered returning to Canada for a bit to think over her next move and then going back to be with Konstantin. If he still wanted her in a year, then she would know he really, truly wanted her. And by contrast, she would know that she wanted him — not the idea of him or the trappings of his lifestyle.

But then, out of the blue, he said those words. Giant, unforgettable words. He was leaning over one side of the counter in a crumpled dress shirt, a cigarette dangling from one corner of his mouth, his eyes on the French press as he poured some black coffee into her cup. That was the moment when he said, with a shrug:

I mean, why don't we just get married?

Héritage

The problem was that Jean never pictured herself getting married. It seemed best to avoid the whole messy experience, if you could. Bureaucratic nonsense, letting the government into your bedroom. Her parents never married. She grew up a bastard child, a badge she wore with pride. Born out of wedlock. Who wanted to be wedlocked, anyway? She'd imagined a few times what her life would've been like if her parents had married, if her father would've stuck around. But her mother was always very clear: we're better off without that fils de pute.

Marie-Georges and her father met in Paris, in Belleville. He was French. He had a petite handlebar moustache and smoked with a French accent. They had a one-night stand in a fleabag hotel and drank cheap champagne together. No, no, he was American. From New York, New York. He was a touring musician and played electric guitar. He was passing through Montreal, and he was very handsome, but bad in bed. He was from Belgium, Switzerland, Monaco. He was a soldier, a thief. La vérité change constamment. Dizzying, trying to keep track of all the stories her mother told.

Jean was eight when she learned the truth about her father after unearthing an old box of photos beneath her mother's bed labeled "Fuck You." Her mother had carefully labelled and dated all the photos on the back, which suggested that her 'fuck you' was, at best, disingenuous. The father she found in those boxes was surprisingly mundane compared to her mother's wild stories. Luc Tremblay was Québécois, and he'd grown up down the street from her mother. They'd gone to the same high school; she'd drawn a heart around his picture in her yearbook. Like Jesus, her father was a carpenter. She wondered why her mother hadn't just admitted this, if she'd always imagined herself being with someone more interesting, more different from her, and moving somewhere else besides Montréal.

Jean didn't remember when her father left for good, but her mother told her she was three at the time. She did remember that afterwards her mother had a string of terrible boyfriends, all of whom she met at the bar where she worked. The last of these, a police officer, stuck. Marie-Georges followed Paul all the way to Cleveland where she got a job working in a bar that required minimal knowledge of English, besides the words: old style, blatz, coors light, jack, and coke. She was proud of how well her mother adapted, even convincing them to put poutine on the menu as a special. Paul and Marie-Georges married, and her mother eventually got U.S. citizenship. But her stepfather was a cruel man. Jean was afraid of his menacing presence, his gun an ever-present spectre in their house, though it never left its holster. She tried to be away from the house as much as possible.

Paul allowed only English at home; this was America, after all. Her mother initially put up a fight but backed off as she started to get sicker and sicker with lung cancer. Eventually, she wheezed every time she spoke and understandably didn't want to waste her precious breath fighting with him. It hurt to watch, how short he was with her, how her mother rasped and coughed, struggling to get words out. Suddenly, Jean and her mother were surrounded by English on all sides, and it became the path of least resistance. She learned English in school, and with her mother's encouragement, soon shook off French like a dog after rolling in mud.

She was sent to stay with her grandparents, Agnès and Gaspard Arsenault, in Maisonneuve every other summer. But the years apart made it increasingly hard to communicate with them. She had to keep asking them to repeat themselves. Every time she asked, they looked at her, heartbroken. As a teenager, she refused to spend all day cooped up in their stuffy, smoke-filled apartment, trying to relearn their language and watching Québécois TV. So she went out, rode her bike around, went to parties, and got into trouble. She would later regret this when both her grandparents died within a year of each other, two years before her mother died. By the time she realised what she'd had, it was gone.

The older Jean grew, the more curious she became about her mother and father's pasts. She decided to go to college in Montreal and to relearn her parents' language. She would do this specifically to spite her stepfather. Mais cela n'était pas aussi facile comme elle l'espérait; elle se sentait comme un étrangèr dans son propre pays. Tout ce qui la rattachait à cette ville était parti. Le français n'avait pas glissé de sa langue, même si elle sait, quelque part dans le fond de son cerveau, que les voies neurales sont toujours là. Very slowly, the French came trickling back. Even more slowly, she got better. But she never shook the outsider feeling, never forgot she was primarily an anglophone.

Her mother left everything to Paul in her will, which Jean understood was about fear. She didn't take it personally; she just wanted to get the fuck out. She knew better than to ask for anything from him and was relieved when she got accepted to college in Montreal and could move out of his house. She took out student loans (Canada was at least cheaper than the States), shipped her belongings, and never looked back.

Even though she'd married someone else, Jean had a theory that her father was the real love of her mother's life, and she of his. They were both just too têtu to admit it. The last time she spoke to her father was to tell him that her mother had died. He didn't attend the funeral but sent along an expensive bouquet of irises and white roses. She started texting him after that, wanting to reconnect, until he asked her to stop. Too much time had passed, he said, he hadn't been in their life, and he didn't want to intrude now and make things complicated.

In light of all this, Jean had made her mind up long ago that she would never be a bride, much less a wife. Her mother's marriage to Paul was perhaps the greatest mistake of her life. She'd seen how much pain he caused her, how scared and trapped she felt. Jean didn't want to risk making the same mistake. Pas de blanc, pas de dentelle. There was also something decidedly uncool and old-fashioned about marriage, at least in her circles.

But she tried to think about it logically. She'd worn herself out trying to devise alternative solutions to her visa problem and kept coming up blank. Now Konstantin was handing her the answer. The whole thing felt like a kind of fairytale, which was exactly why she couldn't trust it. But maybe, unlike Luc and Marie-Georges their story could have a happy ending. She knew, without a doubt, that she and Konstantin really loved each other. What was the worst that could happen?

Enterrement

A quiet, city hall affair. Utilitarian; designed not to intrude on anyone's lives. He bought her a ring for the occasion. Bronze, inexpensive, but she loved it.

Nat, Layla, and Jody would've happily thrown her a hen do (any excuse to go to a strip club), but she didn't tell anyone she was getting married. If they had, she probably would've made a joke about how the French for *hen do* is *enterrement de vie de jeune fille*, which translates roughly as: burial of the life of a young woman. They might have taken this as a bad omen. But no one knew about their wedding, so there was no one there to say anything to her when the panic started to set in. She told herself it was normal, just nerves.

Jean and Konstantin waited for their turn with the other couples, only a few of whom appeared to be in love. The couple directly in front of them were arguing loudly about whether or not someone named Ronda was a cunt. As she and Konstantin moved up in line, they learned that this same couple had been married and divorced several times.

You were sauced last time, the woman said. You called me the wrong name.

I still got you a new ring, though, the man pointed out.

To Jean, the couple seemed like a bad advertisement for their marriage, but she felt very adult as the ink dried on the paper. When she promised to love Konstantin until death, she meant it.

Congratulations, said the clerk. Next!

Significant, Other

After they got married, Jean became John. Instead of her last name, she changed her first. Everyone found this very confusing.

So you're trans? people asked.

No, I just like the name.

You can't be a woman named John, they said.

But I am, she shrugged.

It's not that John had never considered what it might be like to change her gender before. She had, many times. She'd often wondered what it might be like to live as a man in a man's world. She'd often imagined the type of man she would be: soft spoken, a professional translator, trouble maintaining erections. What types of models for men did she have anyway? Her father, her stepfather? She didn't want to be like either of them.

In the end, she always arrived at the same conclusion: while she did not feel entirely comfortable calling herself a woman, she also did not wish to be a man. She knew from her friends and the world around her that there were more than two options, but she'd never landed on a word that felt right to her. Pas en anglais, en tout cas. Moreover, John refused to pick a side. She lived her whole life in-between, gender being just one of many examples.

Nat was the only one who got it immediately because they'd changed their own name so many times. As far as they were concerned, it was everyone's prerogative to choose a new name at any time, for any reason. John appreciated how they didn't ask for an explanation and went out of their way to correct others when they said John's name wrong.

The change didn't sit so well with other people she knew, though. This included Konstantin.

I'm going by John now, she told her new husband.

He smirked, thinking it was a joke.

OK, I'll play along. You're pronouncing it differently? Pretentiously. The French way. Jeee-annn-nne.

This happened a lot. People assumed she was mispronouncing her own name.

No, no. J-O-H-N.

He laughed. That's a man's name.

So is Jean, in some places. Jean Valjean, Jean Genet.

No, but your name is pronounced like Gene.

Ok, so there are lots of men named Gene. I mean, names are genderless. It's all about what meaning we give them.

Well, in that case, I think I'll start going by Katya.

I'm serious, Konstantin. I want to be called John.

I don't buy it for a second. So go on. Make me understand why.

I just don't want... this marriage thing. I don't want to become just your wife, just an appendage, an afterthought. I need to assert my own identity. I've changed since my time in London, I know I have, and this seems like an appropriate way to acknowledge that.

I don't get it. Why John? You have some sentimental attachment to that name?

No, I don't know. I just feel like a John. Or John feels like me right now. Don't you ever feel like something else besides Konstantin?

No. It's my name. And I'm named after my grandfather. I wouldn't disrespect him by renaming myself.

Ok, sure, that makes sense. I don't know how to explain it better. But will you do that for me, as a favour? Will you call me John from now on?

You're so strange sometimes. I can't say I really understand you. But okay. If it makes you happy, I'll call you whatever you want.

He sounded very convincing when he said this. But in reality, nothing changed. He continued to call her Jean.

John was not particularly offended by this. She knew change was hard, and she knew Konstantin loved her and meant well. She corrected him the first few times, then let it slide. She was letting things slide more and more in her marriage. Things she'd never, ever imagined she would excuse or let go. They crept into her life and invaded, English ivy winding around her neck.

It started slow. She would get hungry and start to cook a meal for herself with whatever she could find in the pantry. But eventually this seemed stingy, selfish even, so she would make extra in case Konstantin wanted some when he came home. On the surface, there was nothing coercive about this. But before she knew it, she was cooking for the both of them almost every night, and before he knew it, he was expecting food waiting for him when he returned home. Nights when she didn't prepare a meal, when she was too tired to cook or wanted to order a takeaway instead, he asked if something was wrong.

She also noticed that Konstantin had a habit of draping his clothing over various surfaces — the tops of doors, tables, lamps, heaters (dangerously). He made chairs into ghosts by covering them in a canopy of white dress shirts. It bothered her, and she took to gathering his dirty clothes and putting them in the hamper or hanging the clean ones up in the closet. She told herself this was just a form of kindness, care. He was absent-minded, and she was helping. But the truth was that it bothered her far more than it bothered him, and so she was automatically the one responsible for fixing it.

The same was true when the dishes started to pile up in the sink. Before her, Konstantin admitted to eating all of his meals in restaurants or straight out of takeaway containers, in part because he loathed doing dishes. She'd assumed incorrectly that he ate out all the time when they travelled only because they didn't have anywhere to cook; but once they returned to London, she realised this was simply his lifestyle. Once, John stopped doing dishes to see how long it would take him to notice. After a week, when dishes threatened to tumble off the counter and break, John begrudgingly scrubbed the hardened grime off a few. When Konstantin came home, she finally confronted him.

Hey, I know you're busy. But I don't want to be responsible for the housework and cleaning up all your messes.

You could've said something, instead of quietly seething and testing me.

I wasn't seething. (But she was.) I feel like it was fair to expect you'd do them at some point. It's not my job.

He nodded. OK, no problem. I'll hire a maid.

She looked at him incredulously.

Why can't you just do it yourself?

I've found that doing away with all that other . . . stuff frees up my mind to think about other things. Easier for me to be creative when I don't have housework.

Of course it was easier to be creative when all your needs are taken care of by someone else, John thought.

But someone has to think about housework.

You want me to help out more? That's fine. I can do that.

He looked her in the eyes sincerely and sounded like he really meant it. It was exactly like when he said he would start calling her John. In practice, he never followed through. Every month, it felt like, he built a new tower of dishes, and they would have the same discussion over again, until John got sick of the conversation and cleared the dishes by herself.

He had never, she reminded herself, explicitly asked her to do any of this. In fact, he often asked her to stop, offering to pay someone else to do it instead. But she insisted on completing the chores herself. When she tried to delegate certain tasks to Konstantin, he did such a bad job that she wondered if it wasn't on purpose. She asked him to go to the laundromat, and he mixed the darks and lights together in the washing machine until the colours bled.

John deeply resented their new dynamic, one she'd never had in a relationship before. But she didn't want to complain too much and to appear ungrateful.

She wasn't upset about the housework per se but rather his insistence that he shouldn't have to participate. He struck her as incredibly spoilt. If they were dating, John probably would've dumped him at this point. But Konstantin wasn't just some summer fling or boy she was sort of dating. They were married.

Although they'd both agreed that the wedding wouldn't hold any real weight, it did. The joke was on her, thinking she'd be immune to the institution of marriage. John was realising that deep down, she wanted to be part of a family. Before Konstantin, she was filled with the kind of loneliness that comes from never being truly understood. She kept her college friends at a distance. During school breaks, everyone always went home while she stayed in the dorms studying or went out to sleep with strangers. In the summers, her friends went on trips with their families to lakes or mountains, returning with tans and group photos. John stayed in Montreal and worked. She sometimes made up stories to share with everyone, because she didn't think they wanted to hear about her mopping the restaurant bathroom for the hundredth time.

Konstantin understood what it was like to want a real family. He rarely spoke to his own on WhatsApp, and when he did, it always sounded contentious. When she talked about her distant father, her abusive stepfather, or her dead mother, he didn't look at her with pity like most people did. He knew what she was feeling. *There could be something beautiful*, she thought, *about two people with no real families constructing one of their own.*

And she liked having a partner, someone to lean on when things got rough. To John, that meant they needed to love each other despite their flaws and to work out their disagreements together. She was so used to discarding people the second things became hard or complicated. John was good at running away, but it wore her down. She was tired of running. She vowed that she would do her part to keep the two of them together.

Cette fois, en place de détruire, she would create.

Traduire, Trahir

Konstantin was the one who first suggested that she translate his poetry. He asked her to translate his book изгой from Russian into English because he knew how much she loved translation, and he could see she was bored. John wasn't allowed to legally work in the U.K., but there was no law saying she couldn't prepare some translation samples while she waited for her spousal visa to come through.

At first, she was thrilled at the challenge of translating her husband's work. Translation was a chance to play with words, a chance to test herself. Moreover, she loved his poetry and wanted to do her part to help it gain a wider international audience. And besides, she understood him better than anyone, didn't she? She got to work in her new blue notebook, acting like it was a grimoire, and she a witch casting spells through her words.

The first time she handed over the notebook and showed him a draft of a poem she'd translated, she was so proud. It was a long poem in free verse. A lot of his phrases didn't exist in English, so she'd had to come up with creative solutions. He took the notebook and read in silence. She stood and waited, breathless for his approval. When she couldn't bear it anymore, she asked:

Well?

He sighed, exasperated. He spoke like a doctor delivering bad news to a patient.

This poem — it's not mine. It's yours. The phrasing sounds like you. For example — he pointed to a line he'd highlighted. You describe the abandoned church I'm talking about — which is a metaphor, by the way, but anyway, you describe the panes of the windows as broken. But the meaning has more to do with fissures, and the fissure is important because it relates back to the line about ice. Broken windows, that's not very poetic. So, it's too much of your voice.

John tried, then failed, to hide her disappointment. She'd expected he would have some corrections, but she hadn't counted on the harshness. She immediately got defensive, imagining her translation as a newborn needing protection from the outside world.

I did it for the sound, mostly. Broken fits better with the rest of the line. The *k* sound adds that hardness I think it needs.

He shook his head, starting to get irritated. No, there must be a way to get it all in there together. You can't just give up on the central metaphors of my poem. They're not optional.

I didn't give up. I just didn't realise that part was so essential for you.

Which is exactly my point. You've turned it into *your* poem, filled with the kind of things you say, the speech you prefer. You've stripped it of me. Look. He showed her the poem again. You've used the word *void* like three times. Have you ever heard me say that word? No. That's something *you* say.

She considered. The point was to make the author happy, and if the author was unhappy, she was doing something wrong. He wouldn't pick on her for no reason. She dropped her weapons.

I'm sorry, you're right. Let me try again. I'll do better.

If you want my advice, you need to diminish your own ego. Translating the poem is not about you. You're not editing, and you're not rewriting it the way you like it. You're just saying what I wrote, in English.

John was upset, but she knew he was right. She'd read the poem too quickly, made some rash guesses, and attached her own meaning to it. Every subsequent decision stemmed from her (incorrect) interpretation of his words. Even if Konstantin's criticism was cruel, she knew he meant well. He was hardest on himself, after all. She'd heard him ripping into himself after a reading, saying it was shit, he was shit, he would never do it again. Him telling her she could do better was a sign of esteem, that he had faith in her and expected excellence. She could do better than this; she knew Konstantin so well. Or thought she did, anyway. One poem and now she was not so sure.

She was embarrassed but determined to redeem herself. So she went back to the drawing board. In her notebook, she diagrammed the poem, sliced it up and labelled all of its parts like an entomologist. Then she put all the words, one by one, into English. When she was done, she had an extremely literal translation of the poem. It sounded terrible. So she retroactively added the music back in.

Her first draft of the poem took two weeks, but she devoted four to the next one. She pestered Konstantin with a constant stream of questions to clarify his meaning, and she supplemented this by asking Nat questions and sending emails to other Russians who could provide more context. In every stanza, she made sure to express ideas the way she thought he would, not in her own manner. Anything that sounded like something she would say, she erased. Her job, she reminded herself, was to be invisible. No one wanted to see her dirty fingerprints all over his poem.

But a month later, when she finally showed Konstantin the new version of the poem, his reaction was exactly the same as the first time. He stiffly handed her back the papers, riddled everywhere with red pen marks like bullet holes.

You didn't listen to anything I said last time. There's still too much of you in this poem. The cadences, even the title you chose. I don't think you can help it — you're not a poet. You just don't know how to make something sound poetic.

But I read poetry. Lots of it. And then she added, hurt: You really think it's that bad?

I think it's not ready. In its current form, it's not publishable. The images are too confusing.

Did you read the footnotes? I explain a lot of the —

No one reads footnotes, he cut her off. Assume your reader is not going to look at the footnotes or the stupid translator's note.

Even though she wanted to cry, she nodded. Weeks of work, wasted. She told him she would continue to work on it until he was satisfied.

Silently, she was beginning to suspect that the problem was not her translation skills. As she worked, she felt increasingly constricted by his demands, which grew more and more extreme. She wondered if this was normal for a translator-author relationship. Soon his reason was that a conjunction sounded too much like her, and not enough like his voice. At one point she thought, was that so fucking bad? If the new poem was a marriage of both their voices? He was never, it seemed to her, happy with a translation. No matter what she did. The most she could ever get out of him was:

It's okay.

Sometimes she thought, darkly, that the real reason she wanted to translate his work was because she liked that rendering of him best. In translation, she was alone with just his thoughts, neat and compact on the page. Contained. The book held him, making him smaller, more manageable. In his writing, he was incredibly courageous, sensitive, daring. He was not always all of these things in real life. In fact, there were days when, after arguing about dishes and laundry again, she longed to return to the Konstantin on the page. Him distilled and edited until only the most essential, sparkling highlights remained. And even more than that, she liked the new version of him she created through translation. She liked him seen through her eyes, a more generous and romantic vision than another translator, a stranger who didn't know him so well, might have chosen. She liked to think that in transmitting his words into English, she found a way to make them shine anew.

She'd assumed, based on his reactions, that he would never agree to let her publish the translations, the promise of their collaboration a chimaera. She worried that all her hard work was for nothing, but she told herself that if nothing else, it was practice for her next translation project.

So she was pleased when, in the end, his desire for exposure won out. A few months later, Konstantin begrudgingly agreed to show her translations to his editor to get her to stop nagging. His editor insisted they were excellent and immediately went after the publishing rights. She couldn't stop grinning after she heard back, so pleasantly surprised that someone understood. She was beginning to feel crazy, but this confirmed she wasn't. Once other people praised her work, Konstantin seemed to shift his position. She imagined that the praise felt like it was for him, for how good his words sounded in English. Eventually, they reached an agreement with a British publisher for the English translation. As a concession, she agreed to start going by Jean again. John would be too confusing for anyone who wanted to find her. She also did not want readers to think she was just another male translator. Even then, Konstantin didn't seem overjoyed about the arrangement and especially about Jean's involvement. But she could see the fever in his eyes, the thought of his poetry being reviewed in *The Times*. The book tours he could do, the audiences he could reach, the prizes he could win. She knew he wanted to be internationally known, and he was never going to do that if his poetry was only available in Russian.

When the English version of his book came out, titled *Exile*, it sold better than expected and he achieved minor celebrity status in the London poetry scene. Critics called him a hidden gem, an emerging young poet to watch. But they compared him to Ilya Kaminsky, which she found both lazy and inaccurate enough to be offensive to both. Reviews devoted a sentence or two to praising Jean's "precise rendering" of his words, which she always found strange. Presumably the reviewer was only reading the English version and if so, how could they compare it to the Russian? They were really praising was how acclimated she made them feel.

Her paycheck from the book was barely anything. Konstantin's was not much either, but he didn't seem worried. She knew poetry wasn't his major source of income. She was glad that he provided for her, for them, because without him she would be cobbling together three part-time jobs and still not making ends meet.

Konstantin did a book tour for *Exile* in the U.K. and Jean tagged along, a little dog nipping at his heels, thankful to leave the city. In Leeds, Oxford, Brighton, and others, she was supposed to help answer questions at the Q&A sessions, but the questions were almost never addressed to her. People were always surprised she was his wife, and even more openly surprised that someone like Konstantin was interested in marriage.

You're so lucky, they effused. It must be wonderful to work on projects together.

She smiled ruefully and nodded. When they returned to London, her translation was shortlisted for a couple prizes in Britain. She didn't win.

Jean felt she had done plenty to further Konstantin's career, for very little money. Not that there was much money to be made in poetry or translation to begin with, but she knew enough to recognize that his publisher got a deal with her. So when she prepared to sign a contract for a book of new poems he was working on, to be released in Russian and then shortly after in English translation, she asked for more money, and that her name be placed in a small font on the front cover near his, listed as the translator. Konstantin refused to ask for any change in her original contract, saying there was no way the publisher would agree to anything and she would only piss them off.

This was where all the trouble started.

Jean was fed up with Konstantin's reluctance to help her, and so she did something that scared her a little: she called the publisher herself to ask about a raise and the possibility of sharing the cover.

The phone call lasted over an hour. The posh-sounding man in charge of foreign rights explained the same facts to her over and over, a wall she could not surpass. The problem, he told her, was that customers were more likely to buy books if they didn't know they were translated right off the bat. The word *translation* implied work on the part of the reader. Readers did not like work. They had done some consumer studies. They could lose money by giving her front cover billing, even a little one. Having her name on the title page was more than enough. She imagined him saying all of this from a high-up office, perhaps with a view of the Gherkin or the London Eye. How small the people on the ground must look to him.

The man echoed the same thing she'd heard from Konstantin: make yourself very small, invisible, ideally.

The audience needs you, but they don't want to see you or your work, they said. Your job is all about maintaining this illusion.

But Jean wasn't going to let them get away with that. Nat, Jody, and Layla were always telling her she needed to speak up, to advocate more for herself professionally.

If I never said anything at the tattoo shop, I'd still be the shop girl taking appointments instead of tattooing my own clients, Layla pointed out. Men are only too happy to keep coasting forever.

One of Jody's friends ran a small press that published Romanian titles in English, and every book featured the translator's name on the cover, standard. She saw no reason why Jean, with a much larger publisher, couldn't ask for the same. Deep down, Jean knew she deserved to be acknowledged, even in the smallest of fonts. She'd done her own research. She tried to bring up other studies and testimony from famous translators, prizewinners, about the importance of acknowledging the work of the translator. The man sighed.

Look, if it were up to me, I'd do it in a heartbeat. I'm down with the cause, I get it. But we're a business. In order to stay alive, we have to make hard choices like this all the time. And the fact is that any space we give to you is space we're taking away from the cover artist and from the reader's eyes. My hands are tied. We can do plenty of work to promote you though, when you go on tour with Konstantin. We support both of you completely. There are just some unfortunately backwards issues with this publishing industry as a whole.

She sucked in her breath.

You can say that again.

I'm sorry.

Someone has to be the first to change convention. Can't it start with you?

Again, I'm sorry. Perhaps you'd like to try working with another publisher that is up to your standards.

The next part of the conversation, she couldn't believe was real. She kept revisiting it, second-guessing her memory. She had to have misheard. He said:

At least Konstantin is your husband, so in a sense, his success is your success. You can take pride anywhere it says his name. And maybe, I know, I know, this is a bad consolation. But maybe for now, that can be enough.

There was a long pause. She tried to find the words.

Enough? Enough? Her voice quivered.

I'm sorry, Jean. I know that's not what you wanted to hear. But I really can't do anything else for you. You have a good day.

Silence.

She hung up the phone and screamed into the wall.

Bleu, Saignant

Allegedly, they were celebrating.

Exile was doing well, and so he took her out to dinner at a chic new restaurant in Shoreditch that had just received a glowing review in *Time Out*. Jean wore her nicest blue satin dress. The minute she walked in, she was uncomfortable; it was the kind of place where they gave you the once-over before showing you to your seat. The wallpaper (oh, there was wallpaper) was dark red, almost oxblood, and each table came with a personal mosaic lantern dotted with butterflies. The owner was from Sweden, or Japan, or somewhere that earned him cultural capital. The chef was expensive, and the restaurant was a man.

After a brief discussion, Konstantin ordered them red wine, pea shoots, oysters, pork croquettes, a rare dead cow, and something with ricotta for dessert. The courses came out aggressively, rapid fire, and they had to pace their arguments so that they stopped abruptly whenever the server came near then began again in earnest once he was out of earshot. While Konstantin lectured, Jean seized the opportunity to down her shooter, to spear her fork into the croquette, and mainly, to take huge gulps of wine. The waiter came and asked if they were enjoying the food, to which they both nodded in assent, mouths full. But as soon as he was gone, Konstantin turned to her.

I can tell you don't like the food. Be honest.

It's fine, I just think it's . . . overrated? It's so expensive, and we'd be better off getting something at a chippie.

Это действительно дорого. But you're not the one paying.

She put her fork down.

So? Why do you always have to rub that in?

He sighed.

I just take you out all the time, and I made an effort to bring you here because I thought it would be special. I wish you could at least *pretend* to like it.

You asked me what I thought. Should I have lied to you?

That's not what I'm saying. It just feels like I carry a lot of the weight in this relationship, and you don't even appreciate it.

I do appreciate it. But what's this about weight? You think I don't contribute anything? And anyway, I didn't ask you to bring us here, to order the most expensive bottle of wine on the menu, any of it. I'd prefer if you just ask me how I want to celebrate next time.

All right, fuck me for trying to give you a surprise. It's clearly wasted on you.

His eyes flickered with something close to hatred.

Good taste, in general, seems wasted on you.

Enough.

Trying hard to remain emotionless, she grabbed her coat and scarf and prepared to leave. The waiter caught her eye but immediately looked away. In her years as a waitress, Jean always tried to respect the privacy of her customers and to pretend she didn't see their personal dramas unfolding. But of course you took note of the break-ups, the unhappy couples and unruly children. The waiter stared at them again, and she was not sure whether he was embarrassed for her, Konstantin, or both. But everyone involved knew she didn't belong at a fucking two-top in Shoreditch.

As she stood up, Konstantin seemed to finally realise he'd gone too far, and his voice softened like worn-in leather. He called after her, apologising, adding she was being too sensitive, it was a joke, she shouldn't take it so personally.

She took it so personally. Hot tears fell onto her sweater, and she walked fast to the Tube, refusing to look behind her. Jean didn't understand how she hadn't seen the signs, how she could've fallen in love with someone who was secretly vicious. Il était comme il avait arraché son masque, révélant un visage entièrement nouveau.

She already knew how their midnight dance would play out. The makeup sex, a cathartic release, sweet afterglow. The storm would be over, and for a while, they would rejoice in each other's arms in the calm.

But she knew, too, the way her hatred would eventually creep in again like the slow hiss of gas filling an apartment.

"Don't Stop Believin' " / "Don't Look Back in Anger"

A current of sugary juice and cheap alcohol coursed through her body, alchemy. The booth in neon blue and pink, her second home. The TV flashed the wrong words out of time — words missing but it's OK, she knew them by heart. Her armpits and breasts damp, sweating out the lyrics. The heat of the booth, all their breaths together, the enclosed voices, the bottled noise. She intended to only sing in duos or singalongs, but once there was enough alcohol in her bloodstream, she grabbed the mic and her friends cheered her on. Always the quietest ones who surprise you, the ones who are the most wild and uninhibited in bed. And it was true here, too. Layla stunned them when she belted out old ballads, giving every ounce left in her after work. When Nat and Jody sang together, you could really see their connection, how in sync they were with one another. There was so much potential pressurised in those rooms, enough emotion to lead an uprising.

This was Jean's escape. She was sceptical of karaoke at first, but now she loved coming here to forget the rest of her life. Sometimes she didn't remember the specifics the next morning but the feelings, those stayed with her. The happiness of abandoning herself in excess at the karaoke palace and in the regular trip to the kebab shop afterwards. Nat gently took the mic from her as if it were a baton in a relay race. They started on a pop song while she and Layla went back to the massive binder and picked out another. Jean chose Leslie Gore, "You Don't Own Me."

The irony was not lost on her that, when she finished the song, she had several missed texts and a missed call from Konstantin. He framed everything as concern for her safety, but Jean did not buy this; he'd put her in far more dangerous situations than being out late at night with friends. The songs took on a new, darker resonance now. The Buzzcocks's "Ever Fallen in Love (With Someone You Shouldn't've)" taunted her. Nat saw the expression on her face as she looked at the text messages for the third time and gently pulled the phone out of her hands.

Don't answer him now. We're busy.

Just let me send one text to let him know I'm OK.

Nat sighed but gave her the phone back. She texted Konstantin, reminding him that she was out with her friends and would be home late. He immediately texted back asking what time exactly, and she felt tempted to respond yet again, pulled into his undertow, but Nat gave her a look, and she put it away. Still, the spell was broken; she couldn't concentrate on fun anymore, too anxious about how he would react when she got home. The fear started to sober her up.

Just then, the singing stopped. Nat, Layla, and Jody surrounded her now, forming a semicircle with her in the middle. An intervention, Jean thought.

Nat said, John. Hey. Don't take this the wrong way.

She hadn't told her friends she was going by Jean again. She was not sure why.

We're worried about you. You're always on your phone when we hang out now. You keep reporting to Konstantin like he's your parent. He should trust you.

She knew there was truth in this, which made her fight it.

No, no. He's Russian, maybe it's cultural. He just worries. It's totally fine though.

Nat rolled their eyes. I think you know better than that. I'm half Russian. You know other Russians. Do we all act like that?

No, but we're just different. I don't want to be insensitive to the way he was raised.

Okay. Well, you know if you need anything, we're here. Any time.

Jean looked at her friends. They were so sincere, so concerned for her, and she saw it in their eyes. It was too much. She didn't want their help. She could make her marriage behave.

Thanks, really. But I've got it under control.

They looked at her like they didn't believe a word of it.

Nat especially wouldn't let it go.

He doesn't even call you by your name, John —

I don't want to talk about this anymore. She said it with finality, the edges of her voice icy and flat. They let it go.

Someone said, let's sing Oasis.

Abusive Fidelity

Jean and Konstantin never spoke about having her name on the book cover again. Exhausted by

Konstantin and his publisher, Jean grudgingly signed the contract to translate his second book of poetry. She immediately regretted this decision. He'd shown her drafts of his new poems, and they were — there was only one way to put it — bad. His new poems reminded her of an angsty high schooler after a bad breakup. Gone were the complex, universal themes of the first book, and the work in their place was unrecognisable as his own. It was baffling. At first, Jean suspected her own shortcomings as a translator, her limitations with the Russian language as a non-native speaker. And yet, when she showed the poems to Nat, they agreed with Jean's assessment. The poems were bad, maybe unsalvageable. She tried to broach the subject with Konstantin in the gentlest of ways, suggesting that he take more time to edit the poems in the collection, show them to more people and see what everyone thought. He would not hear it. He insisted that the next book would be his magnum opus, his prizewinner — this was the big one, he could feel it.

This was around the time Konstantin started acting differently. He veered between extremes, either absent or terrifyingly present. He stayed out at bars all night, returning in the morning still perfumed in liquor. Konstantin had always kept a close eye on Jean's whereabouts, ostensibly on the grounds of safety, the terrible things that happened to women alone at night. Initially, she liked having protection and someone who cared that she was safe. But he started to regularly track her whereabouts through her phone when they were apart. If, on occasion, the app showed the wrong location, such as a building next to the one she was in, he would message her frantically until she responded. He would accuse her of cheating on him, and it was on her to prove that she wasn't. That night when he texted her at karaoke was soon nothing compared to all the texts and calls she was inundated with. If she chose to go out and to see her friends, he was visibly upset. He said they hated him, they were bad influences, and he couldn't trust them. Sometimes his attitude was enough to make her cancel plans. If she decided to go out despite his wishes, he picked a fight and they argued until she was too upset to go anywhere. It got to the point where it wasn't worth it, because she knew the ensuing argument would be too exhausting. She surrendered. She told her friends she was sick, and eventually, this was not a lie.

Jean lost weight. The socially unacceptable kind of weight loss; her cheekbones jarringly visible through the soft skin. Her hair began to fall out in little clumps in the shower that Konstantin complained clogged the drain.

The stress materialised in her translations, too. If there was a choice between a more sympathetic version of a word and a more negative one, she always chose the more upsetting one. The tone of her translations started to shift noticeably. She faltered, hesitated when choosing between words, switching back and forth several times, never satisfied with the final result. Maybe Konstantin was right. Maybe she didn't know what she was doing.

When her friends asked too many questions, she started ghosting them, leaving their texts and invitations unanswered. Jean felt blamed for her role in the whole thing. What she heard was that her choice of husband was very wrong, that she was a very bad woman for staying. She became exhausted defending a marriage she didn't even want anymore. She was fading, unable to recognize herself.

Jean had countless words for the disappearing act: *invisible, faint, fading, ghostly, out of sight, obscured, erased, effaced. Seen and not heard, no, not even seen. Not there. Leave behind no trace, residue, fingerprint, fragment, vestige, remains, mark, remnant. Submissive, subservient, subordinate, subject, sub-par, suboptimal, subjugated, subdued, subtracted. S.U.B.: stupid useless* ытсн. *Unobtrusive, unassuming, unassertive, unconfident, un-, un. un(e) invisible. A copy, a mimic, a facsimile, a replica, a reproduction, a forgery, a fake. A woman, a wife, une traductrice, une traîtresse,* переводчица, предательница, *a translator, a traitor.*

So many words, yet they were still not enough. Her world shrank and shrank until it was just a dirty coffee cup, a laptop, and her indented spot on the couch.

*

I would never cheat on you.

That's what he told her, often.

Cheating is the most despicable thing one person can do to another, a violation of a sacred vow. My father did it to my mother, and I saw how it destroyed her, little by little. She was humiliated. If we can't be faithful to each other, we have nothing. He recited this all very solemnly, shutting the book he'd been reading and turning to look her straight in the eyes.

She nodded. She didn't disagree — except for the part about it being the most despicable thing one human could do to another. She could think of things that were worse.

I can promise you that I will never do anything like that to you. Я не такой мужчина.

He said this with conviction, and at the time, she believed him. She believed him then.

*

Night. He was furious and already hard. She could feel the length of him pressing into the thin material of her skirt. In one swift movement, he confidently bent her over his desk, yanked down her stockings and lifted up her skirt. His cock persistent, demanding entry. Her body opened to him; she hated it for this weakness.

The second he was inside her, she was invisible to him. He was no longer Konstantin. He was a business mogul, and she was his secretary, a Serbian woman with jet black hair named Ksenija she was almost positive was based on a real woman. He wrapped his hand around the black wig, pulling at the synthetic strands until she was afraid it would fall off. Riding her from behind, he told her what to say and do, feeding her lines until he was close.

Sometimes there was slippage when he talked fast, and she parroted him too closely.

He said: you are mine.

And she said: I am mine. No wait, sorry, fuck, I am yours.

He said: Do you like my big hard cock inside you?

And she said: Yes, I love my big hard cock inside you, sorry, your big hard cock.

These moments took him out of the scene, and he'd stop everything until she said it right.

When he came, he shouted. Something in Russian that she didn't completely hear, a series of strange sounds. She had a feeling it was a woman's name, but she couldn't figure out the syllables, the sounds remaining fuzzy to her. He withdrew and handed her a towel to clean herself. There had been times when afterwards, glowing, she'd left him on her skin. But in that moment, she wanted to wipe away every last drop of liquid from her insides. She did not want his voice, his fluids, his projections, or anything else of his near her body.

She threw the dirty towel into the hamper and reined in her tears, wishing for the thousandth time that he would just leave her.

Tri/chérie

She could never prove anything. But there came a point when she assumed that he had crossed a boundary, or several. She only had her suspicions, which she tucked away, afraid to look at them directly. She could not ask him outright and withstand a confrontation, and he knew this. But she had a feeling, a woman's intuition. Not hers — her intuition was reliably bad — but a more perceptive woman than herself.

There was a persistent burning between her legs so she went to the doctor. Chlamydia, he said. They gave her a prescription for antibiotics and asked if she was in a monogamous relationship. She said she'd thought so. They said this kind of thing happened more often than you would think, nothing to be ashamed of. It didn't necessarily point to anything. But just in case, she ought to have a conversation with her sexual partner. He needed antibiotics too, or she would get infected again. She hung her head, feeling like a naughty child.

When the nurse asked her if she needed protection, Jean didn't understand the question at first. *We live in a crowded building, so if the neighbours heard me scream, they would probably call the police. Not that the police would help. I have a knife somewhere,* she thought. *I always put my hands and elbows up to protect my face. But he knows not to leave a mark. He's clever.* She took every action she could think of to keep him relaxed, happy. If it came to blows, she knew at the very least that she was scrappy. She'd won more than a few fights in school. But the nurse was right — it couldn't hurt to have some weapons at her disposal. A gun was out of the question. Pepper spray?

Do you think I should get a taser? she asked the nurse, who looked back at her, confused and horrified.

Rubbers, dear. In case you don't want his babies, or so he can't give you anything else nasty.

Oh, right. Jean said, embarrassed. No, I don't think so.

The Offer

The day that everything changed, Jean was working at Hideaway Coffee. She'd managed to convince

Konstantin that she needed a change of scenery in order to work on the translation of his new poems, and besides, it was daytime, and she was not too far from their home. She savoured the last of her cherry flapjack and second espresso, fully immersed in her work. Her laptop had five tabs open: her email inbox, one of Konstantin's new poems, a Google Document of her translation draft, an online thesaurus, and an essay in English that she was writing for a college student.

Around her: a father lifted his son onto the roof of a car so he could see the view, a woman carried groceries on her head, a dog walker was walking a group of dogs that for a moment were lined up from lightest to darkest coloured, a man rode a bike, his girlfriend behind him, her ankle-length boots trailing down, giving the illusion that these were his legs. She'd noticed a difference between translations she worked on at their flat and ones she did elsewhere. The background always seeped in. She found comfort in this, the idea that the city could shape her translation. She was also consciously trying to avoid their flat and get out as much as possible. She thought of *Giovanni's Room*, the claustrophobia created by a small space and a behemoth relationship.

A bright chirp on her headphones indicated a new email. Jean checked her inbox immediately, hoping for a new client. Of course, she technically didn't need the pay at all. But she wanted to have her own money, separate from his. She was secretly squirrelling away her earnings, certain the time would come when she would need them.

The email, however, wasn't from a student. The author was a potential client, or someone pretending to be a potential client, asking about hiring her for a translation. She read the email two or three times, staring in disbelief, unsure if it was a trap. It set off just about every red flag she could think of. But the subject line alone gave her a little thrill: Translation Project for You. Jean was always the one pitching translation projects to publishers, scouting new authors for them *on spec*, which meant for free. But now, instead of her doing all the work to find a job, a job had found her. She hoped this would happen eventually once she gained some notoriety, but she hadn't really earned that kind of notoriety yet, which made the email even more suspicious. She read it again:

Subject: Translation Project for You
From: m.sarrazin@coldmail.ca
To: j.arsenault88@freeworld.net

Dear Jeanne,

I doubt you've heard of me, but I've definitely heard of you. I am an artist based in Montréal. I was in London last year and by chance heard you give a talk at this literary festival, near Elephant and Castle, I believe. You were speaking about translation as mentally and emotionally transformative, both for the writer and translator, all these interesting ideas that I'd never thought of.

I'll be completely honest; before that, I didn't think much about translation. Not that I looked down on it or anything, but I just didn't bother to look into who was translating whatever book I was reading or how the process worked. Ignorant, but I suspect that is rather typical. This is even more inexcusable considering that I live between several languages and am constantly translating myself. What I'm trying to say is that you made me delve deeper into the subject, and I pay great attention to anyone who can make me do that, because it is frighteningly rare these days. Because of you, I came to see translation as a kind of art.

That talk led me to your published translations, well, the ones I could find in literary journals. Your work is breathtaking, full of life. You have such a talented way of reframing thoughts and such sharp, skilled use of language. It reminds me of those painters who can write your name on a grain of rice. Granular, that's how I would describe your attention to details. I promise I'm getting somewhere with this, and it's not all blatant flattery. This is where I confess that my interest in your work is purely selfish; I am in need of a translator. I have a manuscript (currently in French) that I want to publish as a bilingual edition in French and English. As you can see, my command of English is fine, but I don't have the time or desire to do it myself. In light of this, I propose that you come meet me in Montréal to discuss the specifics. I am prepared to pay a handsome sum for the translation and royalties on the book itself. But I need to be confident in the strength of our relationship, which is why I must insist we meet in person. I realise this is a lot to ask, so I am prepared to pay for your flight here and accommodations up front, if necessary.

In addition, I unfortunately can't say too much about myself until we meet in person, as I need to keep a low profile for reasons I will explain later. Again, I know a blind leap into the unknown is probably not attractive to you. However, I think that if you are able to meet with me, you will find that we could make a great team. So what do you say? Are you game for a little adventure?

Amités,
M.

Jean remembered her translation talk well, entitled "Ludic Language: New Experiments in Translation" (Ugh, why had she thought that was a good title? she wondered). She recalled it as a disaster, her ideas not fully formed and her delivery weak, timorous almost. There were only a few people in the room; attendance was usually poor for translation panels and talks. She tried to recall a specific face that might have been the mysterious M. but came up blank. She'd been too nervous to look anyone in the eyes. She was pleased by all the praise, of course. She was used to being, at best, unrecognised and, at worst, excoriated for mutilating a text she'd spent weeks working on.

But she knew she ought to be a little frightened. M. called her Jeanne, which could be a harmless typo or autocorrect but could also suggest knowledge of her past. Stalker behaviour. Still, she didn't sense malicious intent from the author of the email.

As for the offer, she would have to think it over. Agreeing to do a translation for a person she had never met, for a piece of writing she had never seen, for an unspecified amount of money was madness, at best. This person could be anyone, a con artist, a serial killer. She knew better than this. She did. She should delete the email and forget about it. That's what she would do.

She went back into her inbox and tried to locate the source of the email. She managed to trace the IP address to Montreal, but other than that, there was no info available about M. If the letter had been in French, she would at least know the gender of the person writing her. She assumed that M. was a man, although she couldn't explain why. Just a feeling. Maybe she just associated money and bizarre demands with men.

She found herself writing back but kept it brief.

Dear M.,

I'm up for an adventure. But you're going to have to give me more than that. How do I know this isn't a hoax?

Jeanne

She enjoyed signing it *Jeanne*. It felt like the smallest of insurrections, but still an insurrection nonetheless. She told no one about the email. She knew her friends would only try to dissuade her, telling her this was risky, dangerous, self-destructive. She closed her laptop and went home humming a song, happier than she'd felt in a very long time.

*

Konstantin came back very late that night. Nearly morning. Jean's cheery mood was long gone by the time he walked through the door. The celebratory takeaway curries she'd bought for them were cold in the fridge. She decided not to mention the email to him at all.

Где ж ты был? She asked quietly, in a voice she hoped was unobtrusive, feeling like a caricature of the paranoid, nagging wife searching for lipstick on the collar.

Leave me alone. I'm exhausted.

She flashed back to the doctor's office. The diagnosis, the antibiotics. He was likely risking her health, not just his. She could feel herself getting angry and that her anger was dangerous.

Fine. Just tell me where you've been.

Out. Obviously. With friends.

What friends?

Friends you don't know. Россиянам.

They don't have names?

You're starting to piss me off, Jean. Is that what you want to do? Louder again, he asked, is it?

No. I'm sorry, she said softly.

Good. Then just let me sleep. That's all I want.

His phone buzzed. Jean couldn't help it; her eyes were drawn to the screen. A female name flashed, but she couldn't see the message.

Who's that from? She wanted her voice to sound neutral, disinterested. But the tears were coming.

Stop it, Jean. Fucking stop it, right now. You're making me angry. You're always acting crazy, and I don't need this shit.

But —

And then it went how it often did; the train veered off the rails. She tried not to flinch. She wouldn't give him the satisfaction. The tears were coming. Her muscles tensed. The man standing in their kitchen was a stranger. She wasn't sure what he was capable of. The tears were coming. She felt the wind of his movement on her right cheek. The cheap plaster gave a little but did not collapse.

*

Nights like that, when both the possibility of staying with Konstantin and of divorcing him, of emerging from an ugly legal battle somehow unscathed, felt unthinkable, Jean considered ending her life. This was not the first time this solution occurred to her, but the thought was protruding now like an infected wound, more and more prevalent each passing day.

She recognized that her life had been devoid of joy for some time now. True joy, the kind not created by a few too many glasses of wine on an empty stomach until she blacked out. The blackouts were getting more frequent. She could feel it killing her slowly; her brain was Swiss cheese, full of holes, leaking consciousness. The holes in time frightened Jean, her inability to account for her own actions. And now she was reaching a plateau where even the alcohol didn't help. There was something truly terrifying about waiting for things to happen to you.

Her mind was numb. She'd worked so hard to minimise her voice that she felt like she had finally achieved nonexistence. In the dark, she pressed her fingers down on a piece of her newspaper, until the pads of her fingertips were smudged in ink, certain she would not leave a print behind.

*

When she was positive that Konstantin was drunk and fast asleep, she decided to return to the email she received earlier that afternoon. The magic email. Even opening her inbox was tempting fate. Jean realised, of course, that the odds were not in her favour. She was aware that strangers writing to you on the internet out of the blue and promising things rarely mean well. But Jean, already living in a precarious state, was unmoved by the prospect of danger.

There was a new email in her inbox. She opened it right away.

Jeanne,

I don't like being enigmatic like this, but I have my reasons. I wish I could tell you more right now. I wish I could tell you everything, believe me. I've attached your ticket for Montréal. I do hope you'll consider taking it. If you do come, I promise to fill you in on everything. We can arrange to meet in a public place, so that you know you are safe. And I promise that if you agree to do this translation, we will be complete partners in the endeavour. That's the best I can do, for now.

Take care,
M.

There was a PDF of an Air Canada ticket and hotel reservation with her name on it attached to the email. The flight was a week away. Jean admitted to herself that the phrase *complete partners* sounded nice, an ornate dream compared to her current situation. Still, in the morning she called up Air Canada's customer service to ask about the credit card used to make the reservation. M., however, had not missed a trick. The card was registered to an LLC, and she was not allowed any more information than that without providing proof that she was the cardholder.

If by some chance she was still determined to go, how could she get to Canada without her husband realising? This was not a day trip. True, she and Konstantin didn't spend much time together these days, but he still demanded to know her whereabouts at all times. He would definitely notice if she disappeared for a week. She started to look up literary festivals and conferences in nearby cities that she could say she was attending as an alibi.

But in the end, she didn't even need the façade. Konstantin got a call asking him to come to Russia and to help sort out a financial issue of his father's. She overheard him from the bedroom, shouting and cursing and then something that sounded like begging. He came out of their room looking rattled. He was deliberately vague about the details of the matter, resentful when she asked for more information in a way that made her think it was somehow illegal or quasi-illegal. Perhaps this counted as protecting her.

Once they finished talking, he was stressed out and silent, packing in a flurry for Saint Petersburg. He did not ask her to accompany him, and she did not offer. The visa details alone prohibited her from entering as easily as he could. For once, the universe was doing her a favour, giving her a sign that she should go to Montréal while she still had the chance. When he got into his Uber, they did not kiss goodbye.

She checked the time on her phone. The flight to Canada was in four hours. There was no danger of running into Konstantin at the airport since his flight was at Heathrow, hers at Gatwick. Still unsure if she would even go, she began to pack in her own frenzied haste.

She flung open the bottom drawer of their nightstand, looking for her blue translation notebook. She couldn't find it anywhere. There was a deadly churning in the pit of her stomach, the terror of losing a wallet or keys. She'd never lost the notebook before. She was always so careful. Was it possible someone had stolen it? But who? There was only one person with access to the apartment besides her.

He wouldn't. *He wouldn't.* Hysterical, she turned the flat upside down, searching. She made a mess of his carefully curated bookcase, pulling out titles one by one and tossing them on the floor. She opened the drawer where he kept his dress shirts and dug underneath them, her fingers hunting for a spine buried in the fabric. She even checked the kitchen — maybe one of them had accidentally misplaced it amongst the cookbooks — but it was nowhere to be found.

She remembered returning it to its place in the drawer. She was absolutely certain. Was it a mistake? Was he trying to punish her? Would he really dare destroy all her private notes? She liked to think even Konstantin would not go that far. But it was gone, he was gone, and she didn't have any other explanation.

She could only find another small forest green notebook in the very back of his desk drawer. Panicking, she snatched it up; it had to be Konstantin's. There were poems inside and she would need collateral, if it came to a fight. An eye for an eye. He'd have to return her notebook if he wanted his precious unpublished poems back. She stuffed the green one in her suitcase, along with her passport, her hands trembling.

The disappearance of her notebook unleashed something dangerous within Jean. She was on a rampage, bloodthirsty, barbaric. Months of suffering channelled into white hot rage. Konstantin's violence and evasiveness, his possessive grip, the suspicious behaviour, all of it paled in comparison to him taking her art from her. She'd reached the edge.

A long breath. She zipped up her suitcase and sank down on their bed. She was eerily calm now, resolute. She knew exactly what to do. She would steal his writing, she would take one of the credit cards he'd left behind, she would leave the country, and she would cheat on him. To hell with him and to hell with their marriage.

She wrote M. back to say that yes, she was coming. In a dark drizzle, she left for Montreal.

IV. Trouble, Again

Jeanne's head hammers at the temples and back of her skull. It feels like her brain is trying to eat its way out of her flesh. She is too sick to parse real from imaginary anymore. Did the last few hours really happen? Was Violette just an apparition, a manifestation of unconscious desire? Isn't it a little too convenient that she shares a name with one of Jeanne's favourite authors? She wishes she could trust her memory. She can't stop grinding her teeth. For the first time, she viscerally understands the expression *gueule de bois*, hangover. Literally, (animal) mouth of wood. Her throat feels like it is stuffed with sawdust and she can't breathe.

She is still very hungry after the ketchup chips. Alone on the street, she's lost, in all senses of the word. She has no idea what time of day it is, the sun and a little sliver of moon both hanging in the sky. Stranger in a strange land, she startles at her reflection in windowpanes. The pain in her skull feels like the struggle of a new brain trying to burst forth, her Athena.

This is no state to talk to her husband, only a few hours after another woman was inside her, or she dreamed another woman was inside her, but she knows he will just keep calling and texting if she doesn't respond. He's persistent that way. She inhales sharply and dials his number. He picks up on the second ring, already furious.

Jean?

She answers him petulantly, a fourteen-year-old boy:

I guess so.

You want to tell me what the fuck is going on?

Not really.

You're a child, you know that? Грёбаный ребенок. Я женат на шлюха, пизда. I looked at Find My Phone. Сука. What the fuck are you doing in Montréal?

His voice jumps on the other end of the line, static breaking his sentences in half. Damnit, she thinks. She disabled the tracking apps she knew about before she left, but he must have another on her phone somewhere.

He says something else offhand, but she doesn't quite catch it. It sounds like:

I'm going to kill you.

What? I can't make out a word you're saying. She yells, hoping her voice won't sound too angry and set him off.

I said, I'm going to move. The connection is bad.

True, their connection is bad. Fading, she wants to tell him.

Maybe try headphones?

Loud metallic noises. Chairs falling, bowling balls. Something sharp scraping against a wall.

How's that? he says.

Even worse.

Well, it will have to suffice. I can't hear you either and (something unintelligible). Why didn't you tell me you were going to Montréal? Why didn't you tell me anything?

Sorry, it was last minute. I was invited here by a writer who is considering me as a translator for his book. The book is going to be a bilingual edition, French and English.

He wanted you to come in person?

Yes. He insisted.

Is he handsome?

What the hell.

I'm serious. How am I supposed to know this guy's intentions? This whole thing sounds sketchy, to say the least. I know how men are, Jean. им нельзя доверять. You're too trusting a person.

I haven't met him. I have no idea what he looks like. He might not even be a he. He might be one hundred years old. It's just business, really.

Well, still. You should've told me. I'm (something unintelligible).

You had enough on your plate. I figured I'd be back before you even realised I was gone.

You're avoiding me.

I'm not.

And now, how long do you think this is going to take?

I don't know.

Yes, but how long, about?

She's irritated.

It takes as long as it takes. I can't give you an estimate.

Are you sleeping with someone else? Be honest with me, Jean.

No.

No one?

I've never cheated on you.

You're lying.

That's rich, coming from you, Konstantin.

Uh huh. While I'm in Russia trying to take care of my father's affairs, you're off on a trip for some unspecified job you can't tell me anything about. Sounds fucking suspicious to me.

It's fine. Really. There's nothing going on.

Then you won't mind me coming to join you.

What?

I'm flying out in two days. I'm stopping in London first (something unintelligible) meet you. I should be there by Thursday. I already bought a ticket.

But your family —

Things are mostly wrapped up here. I want to see you. We can have a little vacation in Montréal, like the old days.

I'll be busy working.

So take a break. You can't work all day. You'll have to eat sometime.

Not really, she thought. *I could subsist on cigarettes for a week if it meant I didn't have to entertain you.* But seeing no way out of this, she concedes.

Okay, if that's what you want.

And then he's saying something she eventually realises is *I can't hear you, speak clearly*, but she keeps asking him to repeat it because she thinks he is saying *speak queerly*. She knows there's no way he could be saying that, but she worries just the same. Does he somehow know about Violette? Does he have cameras watching her every move? If Violette was a dream, is he reading her thoughts? No, that's impossible. She tries to quell the paranoia, steadies her voice.

I'm saying yes, OK, I'll see you Thursday. Safe travels.

He says something back, but again, she can't make it out. Then the line goes dead.

*

Jeanne's hands won't stop shaking. She should get food and some kind of hydration. Jet lag is kicking in, and she is exhausted. She is almost impressed at how quickly her plane outfit has unravelled; makeup smeared, grime underneath her fingernails. She takes the bus to an old haunt, a dive bar tout pourri and orders poutine, hoping the grease will soak up everything else churning in her stomach. She orders a Belle Gueule, and then two more, because, well, pourquoi pas ? M.'s being fucking weird, and Jeanne's so nervous about Konstantin and what she's maybe done; the more she tries to avoid thinking about it, the more she thinks about it.

Maybe the beer will at least stop her from grinding her teeth into dust. She's the only person in the bar this early, which saves her from the burden of conversation. There's a fruit machine on one side, and she plants herself in front of it, making a kind of loop: choosing a fry, thrusting it deep into the poutine, washing it down with some beer, and playing another round. The fries are very rich even without the gravy. She wonders if they're cooked in duck fat. She doesn't even look at the price. Jeanne's never really been one for gambling, but she has one of Konstantin's credit cards, and she's feeling lucky. Drunkenly, she reasons the least he can do is finance some luxury poutine and a few rounds of fruit machines. He's already coming to Montréal, he's already tracking her whereabouts, and he's already pissed, so what does it matter anymore? She licks her fingers, then presses play. Lights flash, a bell dings, and a glowing fruit salad pops up. Cherries, lemons, oranges.

At some point, a hand shakes her shoulder roughly. She lifts her head. The door guy is pulling her off her stool, growling that it is time to go. Only then does she realise she's fallen asleep. She hadn't slept in more than twenty-four hours. She remembers why she gave up this lifestyle; it was exhausting.

Outside, she tries to steady herself on the sidewalk and fails. Her hair a mess, her skin pale and waxy. Passersby stare at her openly; she's become her mother, the crazy drunk lady. Jeanne wants to explain but cannot find the language to say it. She surrenders to the curb and waits to recover before attempting to stand again. She's dizzy and tries to smoke one of her cigarettes, thinking the rush of nicotine will help. Of course, it has the opposite effect. As soon as she inhales, she feels ill and drops the lit cigarette. Her throat burns, and she thinks she is going to cough, but then no, no — up it comes. The poutine, the Belle Gueules, the ketchup chips, all the shots she threw back the previous night. The inner contents of her stomach appear as she decorates the pavement with her vomissement. Shame flares in her cheeks, as if she is spying on the life of another, until it becomes too painful to watch and she can't take it anymore. She flinches, wanting to look away from herself.

She breaks it down. Where is she? Montréal. She can't recall the name of the neighbourhood right now. What does she need to do today? Contact the author; probably check in to a hotel. OK. She can handle that part.

She remembers that the hotel is paid for already and that she's already missed one night. She searches in her email for the address, then Googles it. The place is fancier than she anticipated. Not like those burned out fleabag motels on Rue St.-Hubert or Motel Raphaël, gone for good. Le Saint-Sulpice Hotel. Saint-Sulpice, just like Perec! Located near the Notre-Dame Basilica of course — typical tourist shit. She decides to go there while she waits for M. to contact her.

She walks the whole way, because she doesn't trust that the motion of the train won't make her vomit again. She has to keep stopping to lean against pillars and benches for support. Her head shrieks from the hangover. For a second she thinks — maybe some hair of the dog would help? But she quickly decides no, give it a rest.

The hotel barely lets her in. The beautiful, young receptionist with neatly pinned-back hair takes one look at Jeanne and cheerily suggests that she might have booked a different hotel by mistake — happens more often than you think. She asks to see her passport, then to see her driver's licence, but she doesn't have one, so they settle on her college ID. The receptionist notes that the room is already paid for by someone named M., but she will still need a credit card for incidentals. When Jeanne hands her one of Konstantin's credit cards, the receptionist raises an eyebrow but says nothing. Jeanne is too worn out and sick to even be offended. She just nods along. *Of course, of course you want more proof, of course you think I'm poor and smell like vomit and don't belong in your marbled lobby. Of course I make you uncomfortable. I look like shit, don't I?*

Finally, she takes the plastic room key, slumps into the elevator, and gets off at the seventh floor. Overcome with relief, Jeanne sinks into the soft hotel bed and considers her next move. M. still hasn't texted. Her only new text is from Nat, one word:

Karaoke?

She leaves it on *read*. A laminated menu for room service rests on the nightstand, and she studies it carefully before dialling the number. She asks them to charge everything to her husband's card.

In under twenty minutes, she is nearly naked, making a terrible mess. She sips champagne straight out of the bottle because she broke both the glasses they sent up with it (the second glass, she feels, was rather optimistic). She's wearing the white hotel robe with nothing underneath as she grabs one shrimp after another and dips them into a generous pond of cocktail sauce even though she is not at all hungry, her stomach still sour and bubbling. She licks the orange-red sauce off her fingers, trying not to get it on any of the white fabrics surrounding her.

In the background, pay-per-view French-Canadian porn is playing. Jeanne watches half-heartedly, dozing in and out of consciousness. She was planning to masturbate, but by this point she's too exhausted for anything to register. The titles all sounded so fun that she couldn't resist. *Le Démon. La Masseuse. Fashion Fucks. Squirt Girl #2.*

She is playing the role of spoiled brat, the wronged wife taking revenge. She tries to emulate her idea of a tempestuous woman. As she throws a tantrum she thinks: *this is good. An authentic tantrum.*

Her enjoyment is genuine; she's never gotten to eat shrimp cocktail before. She cranks the air conditioning until the room turns unnecessarily cool, like a subterranean cave. She hears the blonde in the porno fake an orgasm in French. She selects another shrimp. It's nice.

She remembers to check her phone; there is finally a text from M.

Are you here?
We should meet tonight?

Her heart pounds. She texts back:

Yes at the hotel, thank you again.
Where would you like to meet?

She doesn't recognise the street name M. texts back. When she looks it up, it appears to be a clothing store. A voice in her head warns that it's too suspicious, but she's drunk enough to ignore it. She's supposed to be there at 19h and checks the clock— it's 16h now. That should be plenty of time to clean herself up and to head over there.

First, though, she must finish *Squirt Girl #2* and her shrimp cocktail.

La Sirène

When she arrives at the address M. sent, Jeanne's surprised to find herself in the middle of a noisy party in an abandoned storefront. This is apparently what M. considers to be a public place. Immediately, she feels underdressed and a bit betrayed. What is M. playing at, kidnapping? Although, she's not sure what anyone would want with kidnapping her. It's not like Konstantin would pay a fortune to get her back. But Чёрт, Константин, she thinks. Has his first flight arrived yet? She checks her phone but doesn't see any messages. He must be in the air. She is safe, for now.

Reluctant but reassured by the fact that there are so many witnesses, she enters into the fore, trying to avoid making eye contact with anyone. From afar, she spots a woman with a long braid that she thinks is Violette, and almost turns around and leaves. But then she gets a closer look and it's definitely someone else, someone taller and older. Almost everyone is speaking French, and to her relief, they completely ignore her. She wonders how she is ever going to find M. in this crowd. Probably, she imagines, people think she is part of the catering staff or someone's cousin. She can be anonymous here, which is good, because she is feeling anonymous these days.

She makes her way to a table with a row of champagne bottles arranged neatly like bowling pins, and pours herself a glass of gold. Behind her, she hears a piercing laugh that gives her goosebumps. It comes from a young woman surrounded by a crowd of people listening intently to her every word. She's about Jeanne's age, thin, pale skin, with dark black hair chopped into a messy bob. Kind of punk-looking, with large, expressive eyes, wearing an old leather jacket flung over her sequined dress. The jacket droops slightly, revealing an arm tattoo that appears to be a woodcut of a lion. She also has a small, jewelled septum piercing. This woman exudes a feminine kind of danger that Jeanne does not mind.

As soon as the woman catches Jeanne's eye, she stands up from her chair and approaches without a word of explanation to anyone else. Jeanne had really hoped to make it through the whole party without anyone trying to speak to her. She just wants to find the mysterious Monsieur M., pay her respects, and leave. They can talk business another time; it's too loud here. But now she's been noticed. Is she going to get called out, ejected? She is frozen by the woman's gaze, a fawn flirting with headlights. Elle reste parfaitement immobile.

You made it, the woman says, as though resuming a conversation begun long ago. As if they are old friends reuniting instead of new acquaintances meeting for the first time.

Not knowing what else to do, Jeanne decides to introduce herself.

I'm Jeanne.

She almost says *We're Jeanne* by accident. This wouldn't be a lie. There are many people living underneath her skin. Didn't she have another name at some point? It's gone now, faded in her mind. Jeanne feels right-ish.

The woman breaks into a smile.

Je sais. I'm the one who emailed you. You look just like your photo on your website. I'm M. Ben, Mélusine. Or Mél. Whatever.

Jeanne shakes her head.

I'm so confused. You could have any translator you want, a local translator. Why me?

Mélusine grins but doesn't respond right away.

Like I said, I enjoy your work, and you're brilliant. I can tell that from your translations. For you, they're not just words. No. You have a reverence for literature. That's what I'm looking for. And look at you, you're hot.

She smirks.

Jeanne can't figure out if she's joking. She's picked up that Mélusine enjoys being provocative, that she might not plan what comes out of her mouth. She just likes to say shit and see what happens next. But looking into her eyes, Jeanne's suddenly unsure. Could she really have asked her to come all the way here, just because of a crush? She takes a sip of ice-cold champagne and chokes a little. Bubbles shoot up her nose, burning her sinuses.

T'es correct?

Yeah, yeah, I'm fine. Just confused. Were you ever actually planning to hire me, or did I come here for nothing?

Jeanne's tactless right now. It's the champagne; she can't help it. If Mélusine made her come here for no reason, she is going to be pissed. After Konstantin, she is so sick of games.

But Mélusine continues to smile, unbothered by Jeanne's closed-off body language, the way she clutches the champagne flute close to her chest, like someone might try to steal it away any second.

If you're as good as I think, I have every intention of hiring you. Should I not have said I found you attractive? Désolée. I don't want to make you uncomfortable. I won't do it again.

But after she says this, Jeanne can only think *oh no, no*. She thinks: *I've ruined it.* Ruined what, exactly, she is unsure. She only knows that she liked the way it felt, the warmth she felt when Mélusine complimented her. Maybe this is a good kind of game. Maybe this time, she gets to help make up the rules.

Do you want to go somewhere and talk? Mélusine asks.

What about your friends? Jeanne gestures back to the crowd, now nearly entirely obscured in smoke.

She shrugs. Oh, those aren't my real friends. They're just here for the coke, she laughs.

Jeanne, once again unable to tell if this is a joke or not, nods.

*

They escape into the staircase, arms and elbows scraping against the railings. Mélusine stops at an exit with the sign: "Attention! Uniquement Au Personnel Autorisé." They authorisé themselves and push the door open. Jeanne pauses for a second, expecting the alarm to go off, but nothing happens.

Mélusine suggests they go to Canal Lachine. Jeanne is trying to talk herself out of it — it's late and they're two unaccompanied young women, but Mélusine pulls something out of her jacket. Jeanne can see the silver glint of a pocketknife in moonlight. Looking at her, she feels confident this woman could gut a man like a fish if necessary, they'll be all right.

It's dark, glowing streetlights spaced out like satellites in the night sky. Jeanne can't tell where they're going, completely disoriented. Compared to Jeanne, Mélusine seems relaxed. She is humming some kind of lullaby as they walk. Jeanne wonders if she should ask about book excerpts, contracts, getting paid. But she has the feeling that this sort of talk repulses Mélusine, that she finds it gauche. She will have to go along with it for now.

They reach the canal and bend over the railing to get a better look at the black water, reflections of the moon and stars warped by ripples. Old red brick factories loom in the background, ghosts that will soon be transformed into luxury condos. She's missed the train tracks, the boats, and the graffiti decorating the stone walls. A shadowy figure floats by, and Jeanne is spooked before she realises it's just a duck.

Jeanne can tell that Mélusine wants to jump in. She can see her mentally calculating the distance from the railing, the depths of the water. She pulls off her high heels and starts to mount the railing, and without thinking, Jeanne puts one hand on her arm to pull her back.

Don't.

Mélusine gives her a teasing smile.

Don't what?

I'm not a very good swimmer. If something happens to you, I won't be able to help.

Thinking she's persuaded her, Jeanne relaxes her grip for a second. But as soon as she does so, Mélusine slides her arm away, scales the railing, and dives in. A sleek, sequin dolphin.

The sound of her splash assaults Jeanne, who leaps back from the edge.

She's furious but looks down at Mélusine, who is laughing.

Sorry, I had to. Il fait froid de putain in here though! You were smart to say no.

Jeanne is about to tell her off, but it occurs to her that this is almost the same dynamic as between her and Konstantin. She does something adventurous or silly that he deems childish, and he reprimands her. Elle a de plus en plus le sentiment que toute son existence l'embarrasse. So she makes an effort not to say anything harsh. Instead, she slips over the railing and leans against it, inches from the spot where Mélusine is treading water.

You know there's probably sewage in there.

Peut-être. I bet I'm the nastiest thing in here, though.

How can you say that? You're so beautiful.

Shit. She covers her mouth with her hand. She didn't mean for it to come out like that. But of course it sounds like a declaration of interest. Jeanne is afraid to admit to herself just how interested she is. She hasn't felt like this since she met Konstantin.

*

They leave the canal and climb over the train tracks, then duck into an alleyway, and stop in front of an unassuming building that looks abandoned. Qu'est-ce que c'est avec cette femme et les immeubles abandonnés? she thinks. Mélusine knocks on the

145

yellow stained-glass window in a specific pattern; one regular, two fast, three slow. Sure enough, the window slides open a little and a man's face appears.

Le mot de passe? he asks, and Jeanne looks to Mélusine, because she definitely doesn't know the right answer. Mélusine whispers something in the man's ear, and he grins widely and nods. The door swings open. Jeanne registers that they are entering a speakeasy, or something like it. She's been to some in London that are very overdone, and it always makes her feel a little queasy to play-act another time. Konstantin finds out about them on social media, which does not seem very secret or special. But the one Mélusine's brought her to feels different. The kind of place she could never get into unaccompanied.

The inside of the bar almost matches the dark night outside. A few white candles at the tables are the only offers of light. It reminds her a little of Paris, but a Paris she has never experienced, from the 1920s. In one corner, a man is playing a very damaged piano. Opposite him, a young couple are draped over one another. They are both wearing silk dresses and smoking.

Mélusine and Jeanne sit down in an empty booth. Mélusine's wet hair drips onto the red leather. She doesn't seem the least bit upset about her clothes being soaked, but someone brings her a towel anyway. The candle on the table sits more towards Jeanne's side, so she pushes it into the middle, until it rests equally between them. The orange glow is flattering.

Mélusine is so spellbinding in the light, resembling an art deco poster. Her face makes Jeanne want to say the kind of things she can't take back. Instead she asks:

Would you like something to drink?

Mélusine shakes her head, which she initially thinks means no, she does not want anything to drink, but then a woman comes to the table carrying a silver tray with two crystal glasses on it, filled with a liquid the colour of ferns. Sugarcubes perch on top of flat spoons, forming a bridge between the lips of the glass. The woman smiles at Mélusine in a way that strikes Jeanne as a little too familiar, and pours cold water over one sugar cube, then the next. She stops periodically, then adds a little more. They watch as the crystals of sugar dissolve into the absinthe, until the glass looks like it is about to overflow.

The woman nods and takes her leave. Jeanne is impressed at the wordlessness of the whole interaction and the spectacle of their drinks. Mélusine tilts her glass, swirling in the rest of the sugar with her spoon. Jeanne watches the silver granules slide down to the bottom and dissolve.

A toast, Mélusine says, raising her glass.

Wait. What are we toasting to?

Us meeting, of course. In the flesh. You're everything I hoped you would be. More, even. You're an original, Jeanne.

Jeanne is not sure what she means by this, if it's meant to be condescending. But she hopes

Mélusine is being sincere. She tries to match her candour.

You're... nothing like I expected.

In a good way or a bad way?

A good way. At least I think so.

Their glasses clink, like bells ringing. For a moment, Jeanne forgets where she is. Elle a la sensation qu'elle dort dans un rêve mystérieux. She's a character at the Cabaret de l'Enfer in Montmartre, winged demons guarding the entrance, leading you into the black, cavernous depths, a space at once elegant and macabre where you could witness optical illusions, swinging candelabras, tables shaped like coffins, strange concoctions, and secret, unspeakable things.

Mélusine's hand on her knee brings her back to reality. She's reminded of Konstantin in the bar in Reykjavik all those years ago and immediately pulls away. Mélusine apologises.

I'm sorry. I don't think before I act sometimes. I hope I haven't offended you.

Jeanne shakes her head no, and even though she knows she shouldn't, that it will only lead to certain disaster, she takes a sip of the absinthe. Even with the sugar and dilution, it's strong, hitting all her senses at once. For a second, she thinks her head might come crashing down onto the table. But then she recovers. To anchor herself, she decides that she ought to use this time to ask Mélusine questions, to better understand her for when she needs to translate. The more information she can bring to her work, the truer her translation will be.

Are you from Montréal? she asks Mélusine.

As much as anywhere else, she says, disinterested. The glass throws green light onto her skin. So she is not going to give simple answers. But that's fine, Jeanne herself can't give simple explanations for her past.

You grew up here?

Somewhat, like I said. I've had a lot of voyages, we'll put it that way. I'm a perpetual runaway.

Me too, Jeanne wants to say but doesn't.

Do you speak any other languages?

Just French and English, and a little Arabic. I wish I knew more.

Yeah, me too.

What languages do you speak?

English, French, Russian.

Languages of empire. As Jeanne speaks, she questions why she has ordered the languages this way. A hierarchy? She realises they are also alphabetical in English. The mention of Russian reminds her, and she instinctively pulls out her phone.

Her phone is on silent, but she can see that Konstantin has called several times. A rotting egg bursts in the pit of her stomach. She can't bring herself to listen to his messages, but she knows that the longer she waits, the angrier he will get.

Mélusine sets another absinthe down in front of her, and she looks up from her phone.

You're pale. Who are you talking to? Your husband?

Jeanne's eyes widen, and she puts her phone away. She'd naively hoped that Mélusine didn't know she was married.

What makes you think I have a husband? She feels childish saying it. Why is she hiding anything?

You translated his books. There's plenty of stuff online. How do you think I found you?

I've translated a lot more than his books.

Yes, and that's why I like you. I like all of your translations, especially the earlier ones. Anyway, what's the matter?

Jeanne gets quiet. She takes a sip of the absinthe but cautions herself to drink this one slowly and to not drink any more than this one. She's already in danger.

Nothing's the matter. My husband and I are just going through a rough patch. We don't trust each other.

She admonishes herself immediately for oversharing. Mélusine doesn't seem bothered though. She says, almost as an aside,

I understand. I've been in a situation like that. There's a coldness in her tone that makes Jeanne afraid to ask her next question, but she does anyway:

And you? Do you have a partner? Mélusine laughs.

No, I couldn't be with just one person. Monogamy is too close to monotony for me.

You're poly?

Oh, god no, not that either. I couldn't have relationships with multiple people at once. I couldn't handle that. So much work, so many calendars and discussions. No, I don't really do relationships at all. I have . . . lovers. She makes eye contact with Jeanne as she says this. Jeanne is glad it's so dark in the bar that Mélusine can't see her blush.

I was engaged once, she adds, almost as an afterthought. We broke it off though. Neither of us were ready. She sighs. Jeanne can tell this is an unpleasant memory for her and so quickly jumps in.

I don't think Konstantin and I were ready either. It's bad. To tell you the truth, I've been thinking about getting a divorce.

I'm sorry.

Don't be. I mean, it's a long time coming. He doesn't even support my work. He's always cutting me down, making me feel small.

Sounds like a jerk.

He wasn't always. Or maybe he was, but I just didn't see it.

Not that you asked, but I think you can do better than Constant Teen.

That's not how you say it.

I know, I was just trying to make you laugh.

And Jeanne does laugh, in spite of herself. She appreciates someone trying to cheer her up.

Anyway. Enough about my marriage.

Agreed. Do you want to dance?

This offer strikes Jeanne as inappropriate and unprofessional. But then she reflects; what part of their encounter has been appropriate? The party, the canal, the drinks in the dimly lit bar? She tells herself that if she is going to cheat on Konstantin again, the least she can do is enjoy it.

So she stands up, takes Mélusine's hand, and lets her lead (as if there would be any other option). She dares to rest her chin on Mélusine's shoulder, inhaling the sweet, fruity scent of her shampoo. She can smell a bit of the canal water on her too, salt and mud. She's not sure what exactly she's afraid of, but the fear is powerful. If she focused on it any more, it would bring her to her knees.

In between songs, the man at the piano remarks how nice it is to have someone dance to his music for a change. Then he winks.

La prochain, c'est pour vous, mesdames. Some old jazz song with haunting lyrics. Jeanne recognizes the melody but can't quite place it.

Mélusine, as she expected, is a talented dancer. Confident in her own body and aware of all its movements. But as they start to waltz, drawing closer, Jeanne wonders if this already counts as cheating. How much of their skin can touch on the dance floor before it approaches sex. They aren't grinding but the intention, the intensity is the same. There is a fleeting second — just a second, but it rattles her — where she feels like they are two halves of a single person. That Mélusine is just another Jean, or John, another piece

152

of herself that has escaped. But then it passes, and she dismisses the thought.

Mélusine pulls her into an embrace. Somehow, this feels like way more of a betrayal of her marriage than what she may have done with Violette. Maybe because this isn't just a random person from a café, because she actually likes her.

Mélusine is looking at her like she can read her thoughts. Jeanne looks away.

She starts to feel nauseous from the absinthe, until the weight of her head becomes burdensome. She excuses herself and sits back down. A man dances with Mélusine for a song, and Jeanne watches them move, mesmerised. The way the light catches on her neck and collarbone, her back arching as she dances, as though for a second she is not subject to the rules of gravity. The man says something to Mélusine, and she throws back her head, laughing.

He eventually leaves Mélusine, kissing her goodbye on the hand. Jeanne teases her about it when she returns to their booth.

Does that happen a lot, men asking you to dance?

Often enough, especially here. I'd rather dance with you, though.

She freezes. I'm awful at dancing.

You weren't bad. If you want, I'll teach you some steps.

Jeanne blushes into her napkin, speechless at the thought.

And then, somehow, they are the only two left in the bar. Jeanne has no idea what time it is, but she guesses three or four in the morning. Reluctantly, Mélusine finishes her drink and pays the bill. She orders them a car. It's the first time Jeanne's been in anything besides a bus or Métro in Montréal.

When they stop, it's too dark to tell the neighbourhood. She guesses St. Hénri. They get out in front of an apartment building, more modest than Jeanne was expecting. But the interior tells a different story. Mirrored chandeliers, giant leafy monstera plants that transform the lobby into a garden, and a sleek elevator that doesn't stop with a disturbing shudder every few floors.

I've lived here for three years. I love it, Mélusine says, pushing open the door to the stairs. She ignores the elevator altogether, which annoys Jeanne, who is by now too tired to walk the five floors up to Mélusine's apartment. But she rallies as best she can, always a few strides behind her host.

When Mélusine opens the door a dark shadow leaps out at them, and Jeanne nearly screams. A demon. No, something cat-like. No, it is a cat. A black cat with no collar. Mélusine picks him up, and he purrs and burrows into her arms.

Can I offer you tea?
No, that's all right.

Right. Well then, let's get to it. What you're here for.

Jeanne is terrified of what will follow, what she means by this, but before she can say anything, Mélusine disappears into her bedroom. Jeanne takes this opportunity to snoop around the apartment. The walls are covered in art that she hopes is Mélusine's. Large photographs, some with abstract, ethereal scenes, others unmistakably violent. The work reminds her of Ana Mendieta, playing with boundaries of humanity and nature. Rawness of blood, mud, and immolation. Other portraits are candid images of what she assumes are Mélusine's friends, soft pink lighting next to bare-chested trans guys in brown leather suspenders, a small woman cradling a larger one from behind. Some of the photos appear to be out of focus nudes of Mélusine, and Jeanne makes herself look away.

Against one wall, there is a walnut bookcase overflowing with books. Mostly the cream-coloured spines of Livres de Poche but also some theory, vintage children's books in French decorated with elaborate watercolour illustrations, and a whole shelf of books in English. Tucked between some of the books are tiny little booklets that read in elaborate scrawl: Papier d'Arménie. The memory of the smell inside comes back to her like a ghost; a warm, inviting scent of vanilla. Elle l'associe avec quelques nuits passées sur le canapé avec des amis, avec de gâteau et de la bière pour souper. She realises she liked herself a lot better back then.

On one wall, Mélusine has framed a magazine article about herself from *Maisonneuve*. She leans over and reads:

Mélusine Sarrazin, 25 (?), has a reputation as something of an enfant terrible in the Québécois art world. Although fairly young and new to the scene, she has already carved out a space for herself with her signature erotic portrait photography. Her work is commanding, but not what anyone in this day and age would describe as shocking, a sister to Nan Goldin. Rumours of Sarrazin's 'salons,' that she conducts more like wild, drug-fueled bacchanalias, float around every now and then. Invitations are nearly impossible to come by. She refuses to exhibit her work in museums or galleries, which of course, makes it all the more irresistible to collectors. Acquiring a Sarrazin original is no easy matter, and those who have managed to are tight-lipped about the details. She has shifted mediums in the past few years, dabbling in short films and sculpture. When I spoke to her on the phone, she also said that she was working on a bilingual novel written in French and English. Sarrazin is not professionally trained, and her past is something of a mystery, but she now proudly claims Montréal as her home. Let it be known that Montréal, long a home to the rebellious and avant-garde, claims her back.

There is no photo of Mélusine to accompany the article, only a reproduction of one of her portrait photos, a woman with a shaved head and an accompanying shadow.

She moves on to the kitchen, which is slightly messy; it's clear Mélusine uses it a lot from all the cookbooks lined up against the wall and specialised gadgets hanging from the ceiling. Her fridge is covered in magnets holding up polaroids of people who must be her friends looking glamorous. A ceramic pot holding what looks like a dead houseplant serves as a makeshift ashtray, flanked on either side by weathered tarot cards. The more Jeanne tries to figure out about Mélusine, the less she knows. Even the article profiling her was frustratingly vague about her past.

Finally, after she's had a good look around, Jeanne checks her phone. Nat and Layla texted separately to ask if she's OK and wants to get together soon. They must be concerned about her, she thinks, but she doesn't answer either of them. Konstantin texted a few times, because, well, of course he has. She texts back that she is with her potential employer and will let him know when she's finished. Secretly, she hopes this is never. He responds right away:

How is he?

She assumes he means Mélusine. She writes back, so as not to draw it out even further:

> A woman, actually. She's nice.
> Not at all what I was expecting.

She can feel his jealousy and paranoia creeping in over the airwaves, strangling her. He is upset. She knows she has wronged him, lied to him multiple times. But she is trying very hard not to care anymore. Two cheaters don't make a fidelity. As far she is concerned, their marriage is already over. And she feels like somehow Konstantin knows this, which is why he is trying to hold on to her so desperately.

Still a little drunk, she tries to recall a study she read once in college where some linguists tried to prove that there was a difference in the attribution of blame between English and Spanish. At least she thinks it was Spanish, it could've just as easily been another Romance language. Linguists and Whorfians are always debating how much, if at all, language determines thought. A seductive idea — that some languages are angrier, tougher, funnier, sweeter, more romantic. That you can learn everything about people from their languages.

In the English language it was possible, even easy, to avoid accountability for an action through the use of passive voice. For example, political phrases like "mistakes were made." Were made by whom? No one knew. In Spanish (or French), taking out the agent is possible, but it sounds weird: literally, you get something like "the vase broke on him." Of course, this phrasing is a little ridiculous in English, and the average person would conclude that a vase could not break itself on someone. She's pretty sure the point of the study was that when participants read a story about a broken vase and the agent (the breaker) was removed in both languages, Spanish speakers were more likely to attribute the blame to the man who the vase broke on. Nothing crazy, but it did go a little ways towards indicating a connection between a specific language and thought.

When she first read about the study, Jeanne wondered what the impact of growing up with multiple languages did to attribution. Did you have a double consciousness, and were the two consciousnesses at war with each other? Could you be responsible in some ways and not in others?

Cheating was done. An infidelity occurred.

She keeps rearranging the constructions.

The marriage broke on me.

No matter how she phrases it, it doesn't sound good.

Standing there, her wedding ring suddenly feels heavy. She takes it off and puts it into her jeans pocket, making something real that she knew emotionally long ago. She knew when she left for Montréal, she knew when she cheated on him. Dans son coeur, elle est déjà partie.

Mélusine finally returns to the living room carrying a large stack of papers. The manuscript. She presents it to Jeanne, who is sitting on the couch. She stares expectantly, awaiting her reaction. The papers are not stapled or paperclipped together and a few flutter to the ground. Mélusine hurries to retrieve them.

Oh, yes. Thanks.

It's not done. But I figured you'd need a while to get through this part.

Honestly, I don't usually translate manuscripts before they're finished. I like to read the entire thing at least once.

I understand. But this is all I have for you, and besides, even I don't know how it's going to end.

She sighs. All right. I'll see what I can do.

I knew you'd understand, Jeanne.

She intertwines their fingers.

Jeanne starts to get afraid. She is too close to starting something she is not prepared to finish. She stands up, still holding the manuscript.

I should probably go, she says, although she has nowhere to go.

It's the middle of the night.

Jeanne knows she can't stay. She should be the adult here, try to keep their relationship a professional one.

Really, I'll be fine.

Mélusine stands up as well, levelling the space between them. Now they are neck to neck.

No, I insist. You're my guest; this is the least I can do after making you come all this way. I'll make up the sofa bed for you. And I'll cook you crêpes with lemon and sugar in the morning, my specialty.

Mélusine... Jeanne starts, determined to lecture her about how unprofessionally she is acting, to stop this speeding train before it runs them both over, to get her promise no lines will be crossed, everything will stay inside its proper container. But even though she doesn't finish the sentence, Mélusine seems to intuit the rest.

She pulls close to Jeanne, and whispers:

Don't worry, I'm not going to fuck you yet.

Then she turns away, emotionless, and starts to fold out the couch. It's as if all heat has gone out of Mélusine's body and entered Jeanne's. There is a shiver that won't leave her spine, goosebumps on her arms that won't go down. Her cheeks flush red red hot. She is too stunned to say a single word.

After Mélusine says goodnight and goes into her room, Jeanne lies awake on the fold-out couch, staring up at the ceiling. Trying to figure out just what is going on with her life, just where she veered so catastrophically off course. Or is she finally on course? La plus belle femme qu'elle ait jamais vu, qui est maintenant sa patronne, dort dans la pièce à côté d'elle. À quoi peut bien penser Mélusine? Is her heart also colliding into her ribcage?

By now her phone is dead, so she plugs it in and waits for it to revive. This buys her some time to ignore Konstantin. She knows that he is obsessing right now, thinking of nothing *but* her and her disobedience. She knows that his rage will only spiral, the longer she makes him wait. She will have to face him sometime.

After an hour or so of being unable to sleep, she turns on a small lamp in the living room and starts to read through the novel. Once she starts, she can't stop. The story is about a young female artist, maybe Mélusine herself. Her prose is very sensual, rich with erotic imagery. Jeanne is turned on by the sex scenes, then confused by her arousal, then turned on again. Her pulse soars, blood pumping through her body faster and faster. She believes that the passages are about Mélusine having sex with someone who is not her, and whether real or imaginary, she is jealous. She reads until the area between her legs feels hot enough to set off a fire alarm and she has to go into the bathroom and splash cold water on her face.

She has no idea how she is going to capture the beauty of these lines in English but can't wait to try. She gets up and rummages for a pen in her bag. Starts to make notes in the margins. She hasn't felt this kind of all-consuming fervour working on a translation since college. She's taken back to the days of endless cups of coffee and cigarettes as she pushed herself to get a messy first draft done before sunrise. She's writing Mélusine a kind of a love letter in the margins, writing for her eyes alone. The cat rubs up against her side, purring, pleased to have a nighttime companion.

Together, they stay up pawing through the pages of the manuscript.

*

When Jeanne wakes up, she has pen on her face. She must have passed out taking notes. She looks around for Mélusine, who is gone. A cursive note on the kitchen table explains that she's off to run some errands. She's left the promised crêpes with lemon and sugar on a plate for Jeanne, carefully decorated with raspberries and slices of lemon. They are still warm, fragile tendrils of heat rising into the air. There's also a paper cup with an Americano inside, although it's lukewarm — she must've bought it a while ago. Is the choice of an Americano for Jeanne, instead of espresso or cappuccino, some kind of pointed remark? Does she think of her as américaine? No, she is being paranoid; she decides not to take the coffee too literally.

Feeling a bit like a thief, she opens Mélusine's fridge and looks for creamer. The contents of the fridge are bizarre, an art project in itself; single-serve yoghurts, apple sauce, condiments, pre-packaged peanut butter and jelly sandwiches. She locates a bloated container of almond milk at the very back and sets it on the counter. *Shake me!* it demands.

The Americano is okay, just okay. The crêpe, however, is one of the best things she's ever tasted. Sweet, pleasantly bitter, and light. The brightness of the lemon greets her, wakes up her senses. Her impulse is to devour the whole thing immediately, but instead she forces herself to take her time, to savour it.

After breakfast, she takes advantage of Mélusine's absence to snoop a little more. She tells herself this is about safety but inwardly knows it's just filthy curiosity. She enters Mélusine's bedroom. The walls are a cool blue broken up by strings of white fairy lights. The centrepiece of the room is a large mahogany dresser with an ornate framed mirror. Jeanne notes that the mirror would make it possible to watch oneself having sex in her bed, then orders herself to put this thought out of mind.

The dresser doesn't tell her much. It's covered with a variety of jewellery, a stuffed elephant souvenir, and dried flowers. Craft supplies: paints, pencils, stickers, glue, glitter, a strange sculpture made of red popsicle sticks melded together in one giant clump. On the right side there's a closet overflowing with clothes, and little stuffed animals on the floor that must belong to the cat. Jeanne is careful not to touch anything.

In one corner is a door that must open to another room. She tries the doorknob, but it is locked tight. Why? Possibly, she thinks, the door connects to another apartment or a back staircase, as sometimes happens in Montréal. And yet the positioning doesn't quite make sense. She remembers that the front door to the adjoining apartment is positioned to the left of Mélusine's door, so there is no one else on this side. Maybe it is just a storage closet, or a place to keep her art supplies? There is no way to know without asking her, which Jeanne feels would be intrusive, more intrusive than she has already been. Mélusine could be back any minute now, and she doesn't want to get in trouble.

Jeanne decides to head back to the hotel. There is a renewed spring in her step, a hope. She can't believe Mélusine is real and that she has an excuse to talk to her again. Reflexively, she checks her phone again. Nothing, not even from Konstantin this time. She's being foolish; it's too early. Mélusine is probably busy doing whatever she does all day — her art? She doesn't text her even though she desperately wants to, because she doesn't want to seem clingy. She feels like a schoolgirl with a crush, embarrassing, overflowing with emotions. She has to stop. Elle devait canaliser l'énergie sexuelle dans autre chose. She needs a release.

Then she spots it: a painted image of a skull next to the words TATOUAGE ET PERÇAGE. Before she can talk herself out of it, she pushes the door open. Inside, one bald man and another with a ponytail look up from their work. The ponytail ignores her entirely and goes back to tattooing a large expanse of thigh, but the bald man makes eye contact and gives her a nod. He tells her someone will be with her in a minute. She studies the flash on the walls: naked women, lucky dice, horseshoes, angels, demons. Canadian tattoos: maple leaves, the fleur-de-lis in blue and white, hockey team logos. In a few moments, a girl with rainbow-coloured hair and plugs asks Jeanne how she can help her. Jeanne initially thinks she ought to get a tattoo, but then her eye catches on the silver jewellery in the glass case up front.

I want to get something pierced. She says to the girl, testing out how it feels to say the words.

OK . . . what do you want to get pierced? The girl looks bored.

Jeanne isn't prepared for this. She panics, searching the girl's face for ideas. She has her nose, eyebrow, and lip pierced, and an industrial piercing at the top of her ear. None of these appeal to Jeanne. But then she figures it out. Smiling, she opens her mouth wide and points to her tongue.

*

It's over in a matter of minutes. She signs some paperwork, promising she is over eighteen. The bald man sticks his gloved hand inside her mouth, stabs the soft of her tongue, and leaves behind a small silver ball. It hurts considerably less than she imagined. There is no blood. Nevertheless, she does feel a rush of

166

adrenaline before, during, and after. He hands her a piece of paper with instructions for aftercare that she throws in the trash as she walks out the door.

She finds a shop window and examines herself. So dumb, so '90s, so unlike her. *J'adore*. Her tongue is numb, swelling a little, filling up her small mouth. When she talks, she has a bit of a lisp. She can't stop pressing it onto the roof of her mouth, rolling it around, gazing at her reflection. She spends the rest of her walk back to the hotel in a blissful daze, satisfied with her plan to distract herself from thinking about Mélusine.

When she gets back to her hotel room, she sits crossed-legged on the bed, logs on to the Wi-Fi and checks her inbox. There are two new messages, and she reads the most recent one first. It's from one of the students, about the essay she turned in a few days ago. She can feel rage tearing through the screen.

> What the fuck did u send me?

it reads...

> This is all in Rusian or something.
> i can't turn this in.
> Refund my money now bitch
> or your going to be in big trouble.

At first, she assumes this is a joke or an unhappy client just trying to recoup his loss. Occasionally students try to tell her they are unsatisfied with her work after they've turned it in and gotten the grade they wanted, in the hopes that she will give them back some of the money. This happens a lot if they get caught cheating, but she always says too bad, not my fault. You should've been more careful.

But when Jeanne opens the file, the text is in Cyrillic and she realises that yes, she must have somehow written the entire essay in Russian. She scrolls down the pages in disbelief, highlighting and unhighlighting the text as if that will reveal something. She doesn't get it. How could she not have noticed a thing like that? Immediately, John writes the student back with an apology and refunds his money.

Now anxious, she opens some other recent essays. They are all in English, she sees with relief. She's about to close the tabs when she notices a bunch of diacritical marks across one essay. A typical sentence reads: *Napoléon revolutionised wârfare and šhaped mìlïtary púrsuîts før dečades to çömē.* Another proclaims: *Perhäpś híš gréâtest cõntribution to mịlitary strátegy wãs the bròader use of årmÿ dîvisíons, knówn ås the côrps d'armëe.* And further down: *Thë chàractèrization of Nàpoleøn as shørt ịs lârgely repórted tö be úntrue, ánd he wäs well wìthin cônventional hèight fór this tïme périòd.*

At the bottom, she's made borders out of misplaced quotation marks, French and English ones:

John squints, trying to tell if the marks are out of place or if she is overthinking it. She wipes the screen with a tissue. No, the marks are still there. Some of them, Jean realises with a shock, aren't French, English, or Russian. What was she doing? How could she not have noticed when she had to have used special shortcuts or keystrokes to make them appear? For a fleeting second, she wonders if she's been hacked. But what kind of hack is that? What purpose could it possibly serve?

And then, when John glances at her text messages, she realises the problem is even worse than she could have imagined. She is scattering diacritical marks like pieces of confetti. Especially in places they do not belong. Jeanne starts to worry she is coming apart at the seams, unmoored, her mind unravelling.

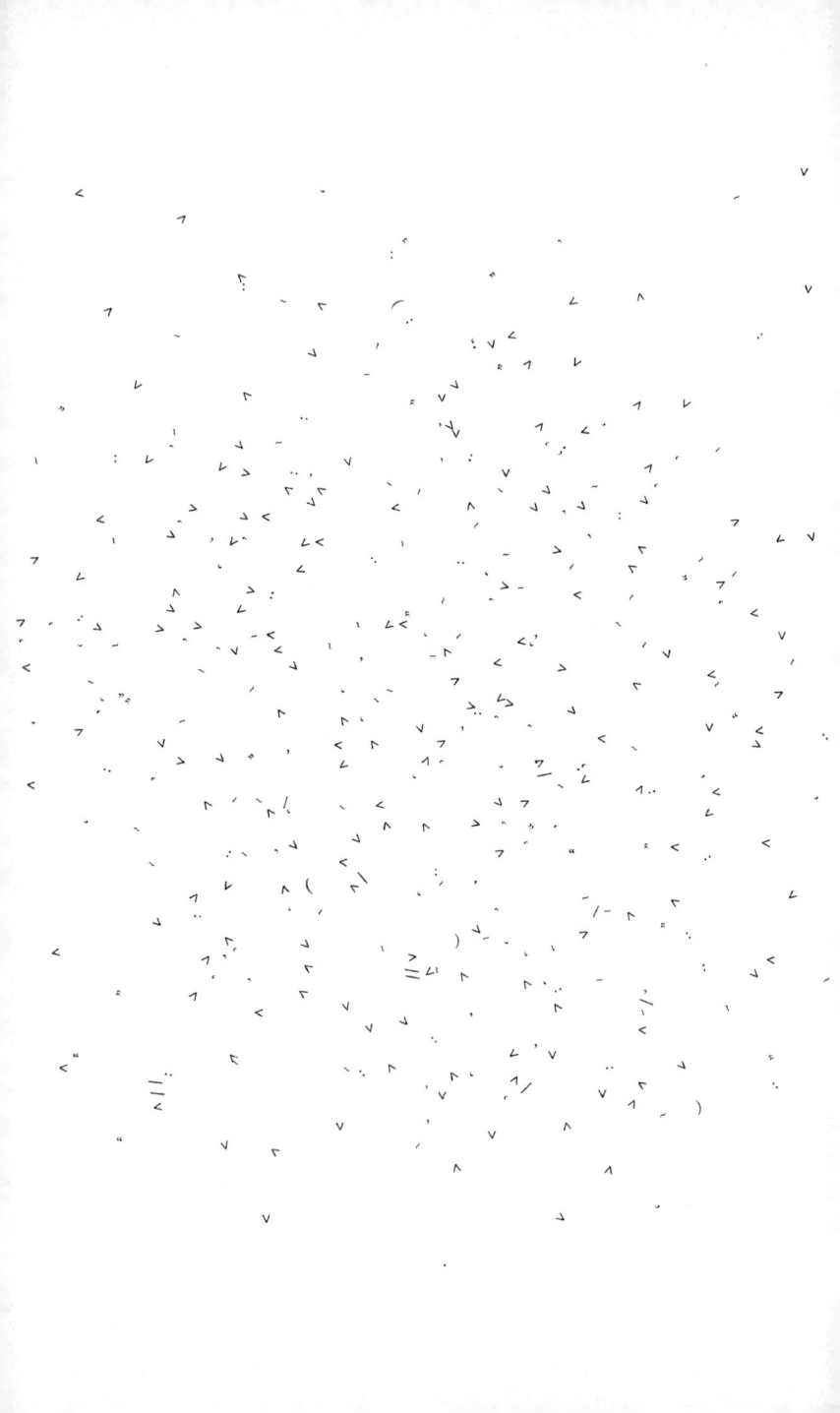

Jean can't deal with this right now. На одну проблему больше, чем нужно. Elle devait l'éliminer jusqu'à ce qu'une bonne решение se présente. Ей стыдно за то, как ситуация делает её непрофессиональной и неловкой. Merci à dieu, ce n'était qu'un студент et des textos, pas une soumission pour un livre. Но ситуация не devait повториться. Elle это обеспечит. Она должна comprendre с проблемой и её исправить. Это всё. Должно быть какое-то logique объяснение всего этого. Elle решает не доверять себе plus, чем нужно сейчас, а действовать осторожно. John will refund anyone else who writes her, no questions asked.

She opens the second email, praying it is not another angry student. No, it's her old friend Clémentine, Clém for short. She remembers vaguely that she emailed Clém from the airport, telling her she'd be in town for a bit. That feels like ages ago now. Clém is from Montréal, and they used to hang out sometimes during her summers there, and then even more when she moved there for college. She is one of the few people Jeanne made some effort to keep in touch with over the years. She knows that Clém was in Vietnam for a while staying with family but is pretty sure she is back in Montréal now. She reads:

Hey, Jeanne!

What a surprise to see your name pop up. It's been a while. Things are good here, just crazy busy, as usual. I've been commissioned to do a series of PSAs for the public library, of all places, and it's been both fun and a huge challenge. I'll have to show you some of the samples.

Anyway, yes of course, would love to see you if you're in town! I don't think I have your number anymore, but mine is the same as always. Text me when you're here and we'll figure out a time. Can't wait to catch up.

xo
-C

Just reading the email improves Jeanne's mood a little. Even if she is losing her mind and her language, there is at least one person who seems genuinely excited to see her. She remembers how warm and calm Clém is and responds right away, double and triple checking the text for marks before she dares to send it. Her own words on the screen look strange to her now, the white letters against the blue background suddenly hard to read. Clém texts back shortly, and a jolt runs through her as she reads the speech bubble. She tries not to think about her Russian fuck up; she probably just needs to catch up on sleep. The bigger picture is this: She's made it to Montréal, she's made contact with Mélusine, who is better than she'd ever dreamed, she doesn't have to see Konstantin yet, and she can spend some time with her old friend soon. She breathes in deep. Everything will be OK. They make a plan to meet by the cathedral in an hour.

She waits outside the Notre-Dame Basilica, ignoring the rain clouds in the distance. A crowd of tourists gathers by the entrance, the stained glass painting their faces like aliens. The windows at the top remind her of sunflowers; yellow, blue, and red petals pressed into a gold background. Their guide explains that the Notre-Dame Basilica was modelled after the more famous one in Paris.

Luckily, we don't have any hunchbacks or gipsies in ours, he adds, to moderate laughter. Jeanne grimaces.

If she were to tell it, the Notre-Dame Basilica is not a replica at all. It was built in the 1800s by different architects, reflecting different aesthetic viewpoints. The guide is expressing the French view perhaps, the one in which the world is centred around France.

Across the street, an old man wearing a fisherman's cap is painting the cathedral in watercolours. Jeanne watches him work, concerned for the fate of his painting once the rain comes. A few more paintings for sale lie at his feet; all the greatest hits, Now That's What I Call Montréal: Mont-Royal, Jean-Talon Market, Old Montréal, Canal Lachine, and the Biodome which always makes Jeanne think of Epcot. The man squints as he makes careful strokes. It occurs to Jeanne that the tour guide might see his art as a copy of a copy, a long echo. But Jeanne sees herself in his painting. A sketch with no origin.

The sky opens and it starts to rain. The old man hastily puts his paints away, shoving the still-wet painting under his jacket. Like the rest of the tourists, Jeanne walks into the Basilica. She puts her money in the box, lights a white candle, and makes her wish. Elle regarde la flamme vaciller, influencée par le moindre mouvement. She is silent the whole time, weighed down by her thoughts.

Jeanne doesn't think of herself as religious. Yet she likes the totality of it all; the different origin stories about how the world was created. Mystic eggs and cows licking giants and turtle shells. The trauma of compulsory Catholicism is still inside her. She can't rid herself of it, but she's learned how to let other elements in.

She thinks about how the most translated book in the world is the Bible, and so many of the first translators claimed to translate the word of God for mortals. The immense pressure and hubris involved in the act of translating a deity. People weren't afraid of translation back then; they felt it necessary for their survival. She thinks about Joan of Arc (née Jeanne d'Arc), turning her visions into missions for the French people. What was crazy was that they actually listened to her. No one listens to teenage girls now, she thinks, especially poor and uneducated ones.

After about fifteen minutes, the rain gives up, like a toddler with a temper tantrum that has cried

174

itself out. She heads out of the church and onto the sidewalk, sensing someone behind her. There is a light tap on her shoulder.

She turns around and flinches, expecting Konstantin.

But no, it's Clém, of course. She's absolutely drenched, holding her rainy bicycle. Jeanne smiles and gives her a wet hug.

Sorry, I'm late! It seemed like every other street was closed for construction and then the storm slowed me down, because I didn't want to get a flat tyre. Anyway, it's so good to see you!

Likewise. Like, you don't even know. Clém fixes her with a serious look of concern.

I was shocked to hear from you, honestly. But it was a pleasant surprise. Tell me, what's going on with you? I haven't heard anything since you moved to London.

While Clém locks up her bike, Jeanne decides whether or not to lie to her.

When she returns, Clém offers to go inside the cathedral, but Jeanne tells her she's already walked around, and anyway it's really just fun when you're a visitor.

Not at all. I come here a lot to draw. Lots of good people-watching.

She likes Clém for this exact reason. She sees the good in things but not in a fake or forced way. She is good at reminding her of a different perspective when all feels lost.

175

Also, I'm sorry this is rude, but did you always have your tongue pierced, or am I nuts?

Yeah, it's new, I just got it.

Clém laughs and grins. Very cool! I always wanted to get my nipples pierced, but I never got up the guts. I'm just so afraid of the pain.

Jeanne looks at her in surprise. She would've guessed Clém had piercings but not there.

Your nipples?

Yeah, my ex-girlfriend had them and . . . well, that's a story for another time. Did it hurt when they did it?

No, not really. It's pretty swollen now though. In fact, it's making it hard to talk, but she pushes through. Clém nods.

Yeah, we should get you some ice chips to chew on.

They decide to find a café for a late lunch, early dinner. Clém says she knows a good sandwich place nearby but doesn't remember the name, only that it has a red awning. They wander the streets, paying particular attention to all the awnings. Jeanne can hear herself laughing; she feels lighter around her old friend.

Transformed back into delinquent teenage girls, they split a pack of cigarettes and start chain-smoking, their voices louder with each cigarette. They never find the correct red awning and instead settle on a small bistro with outdoor seating. The rain is drying up, and the waitress hastens to wipe down some chairs so they can use the terrace.

As soon as they sit down Jeanne starts to get nervous; she's still not sure how much to reveal to Clém. Can she tell her about Mélusine, or will she think she's awful for wanting to cheat on her husband (again)? Should she tell her about the abuse (does it even count as abuse?), or will that freak her out? Above all, Jeanne does not want to be judged right now.

She tries to keep the conversation off herself as long as she can. She asks Clém about her freelance illustration, her project with the library, and the graphic novel she's working on. They talk about her partner, Simone, who does social media marketing for a large fashion company. Clém tells her they got married a couple of months ago because Simone's job has really good health insurance. They talk about her kitten, her awful landlord, her queer Asian book club, all the drama at the queer Asian book club, and who isn't speaking to whom anymore.

When their food comes, Clém says:

Wait, what about you?! I haven't asked you anything, I'm sorry. What have you been up to? Why are you back? How long are you staying?

Jeanne feels her heart rate spike. She takes an unnecessarily long sip of water. She bites into her sandwich but is no longer hungry. Clém continues to look at her expectantly.

Yeah, yeah, I've been good. Here for work. A translation assignment. I met with the author yesterday.

Oh wow! So cool. Do you like the person?

Yeah, she says, trying not to blush. She's great. She's a photographer, actually. I don't know if you'd have heard of her? Her name is Mélusine Sarrazin. Clém nods.

Actually, I think I have? I feel like I've been to a show that she was in before. I've never met her, though. She's pretty young, right? Like twenty-three or something. But bravo, that's amazing!

Yeah, it's been cool.

How are things otherwise? Are you thinking of staying in London?

I guess. I don't think I would move back here, if you know what I mean. It's not like I've really stayed in touch with anyone besides you. It felt like once I graduated college, everyone kind of iced me out. Clém arches her eyebrow.

Is that how you remember it?

Yeah?

I don't know what reality you're living in, but no one ever iced you out.

I just always felt like everyone besides you was judging me for not growing up here, and the second I left, they were free. They didn't have to pretend to like me or to be my friend anymore.

That's not what happened at all. People kept asking me what your plans were, and you just went to

178

Iceland without telling anyone except me, I guess. You stopped responding to their texts. Everyone was worried. That's why I was so surprised to hear from you.

Jeanne sputters, closes her mouth. This is not the first time someone has told her this, and it hurts.

I don't . . . I mean I guess I could have . . .

Look, it's OK if you were too busy or didn't want to talk. But you shouldn't go around saying that everyone rejected you, when it was kind of you who rejected them.

Jeanne knows this is her pattern. She moves, she crosses a border, she becomes a new person and discards her old friends in order to make a clean break. She tries hard not to think about the collateral damage.

I've kept in touch with you though, right? I've tried at least. Things have just been so chaotic.

No, no totally, I get that. Things have been chaotic for me, too. Simone is trying to convince me to move somewhere else because of our shitty CAQ government. Their laws are really fucking xenophobic, I'm sure you've heard.

Ah, but we must protect the French language! Jeanne jokes.

In reality, she loathes this obsession with treating the French language like a damsel in distress. It's all a lie, as she learned in her linguistics classes in college. Traces of colonialism hidden everywhere in their French, words stolen from Indigenous languages.

The name of Québec itself is an Algonquin word for a narrow strait, referring to the St. Lawrence River. Not to mention Little Portugal, Little Italy, Chinatown, all the neighbourhoods of immigrants who came to Montréal seeking refuge. The robust Yiddish and Hebrew that blew into your face as you walked into Mile End, blending with the smell of rye bread, briny pickles, and smoked meat. Her mouth waters for language.

French can go to hell for all I care, Clém scowls.

I mean, I don't disagree, and I use it every day. You're really thinking about leaving though? Where would you go?

Well, that's the issue, isn't it? How do I know somewhere else would be any better? It's just been getting so expensive to live here. And it just feels like everything is becoming more racist. Now you can't even wear a headscarf and be a teacher. Simone has family in Australia so she brings that up a lot, and she doesn't like the cold, but I don't know if I'm ready. I don't know if I'll ever be ready for that. But she's really homesick. You know, they have cockatoos there.

What? Jeanne is not expecting that sentence.

Like how we have pigeons just wandering around everywhere, they have that in Australia but with cockatoos. That's wild to me. So I get why she misses it. I'd like to visit sometime. But I don't want to live there. Her face turns serious. Things are complicated. I don't know, we've been arguing about it a lot.

Clém's eyes unfocus as she looks off into the distance, as though it might provide her with an answer. In the silence, Jeanne lets out a sigh of exhaustion thinking of her, and all of them who have to constantly make these calculations and recalculations about gender and sexuality and race and safety and money and healthcare and citizenship and and and...

Anyway, weren't you seeing someone in London, last time we talked? How's that going?

Jeanne tenses. She is unsure how to explain the past few years. How to tell her that the relationship is sucking the life out of her, that she is afraid of what he will do when he finds her. She was planning to lie to keep things simple, but after a glass of white wine, her guard is down.

Yeah, I'm seeing a man named Konstantin. He's Russian, a poet. We actually got married.

Oh! Well congratulations, sorry I didn't know. Jeanne shakes her head.

No one knew. It was mostly so I wouldn't have to leave the country. I mean, I did love him. But things are bad between us, right now, to be honest.

Clém looks at her carefully, trying to figure something out. But she doesn't say a word, just patiently waits for Jeanne to continue.

I know this sounds dumb, but he's a different person than when I married him. It feels like he kind of hid who he really was from me, and I don't like the real him.

Ugh, I'm so sorry. That's tough. Has he ever tried therapy?

Jeanne laughs bitterly, years worth of bitterness. She shakes her head.

He would never agree to something like that. He thinks talking about your feelings is a huge weakness.

Sounds very Russian of him.

Ha-ha. No, the problem is not that he's Russian; it's that I think he doesn't love me anymore either. And he holds everything inside, and sometimes he gets violent. Like he scares me sometimes.

Jeanne can feel herself about to cry. She pictures a hole in a dam, forcing her finger in the hole, plugging it up. She inhales sharply. In answer to a question Clém hasn't asked, she says,

I don't know if I'm ready to talk about it.

Clém nods and wordlessly pulls her in for a hug. With almost anyone else, Jeanne would've resented this gesture and flinched, but she's known Clém forever and her body relaxes into the embrace. Since she can't find the words, Clém pulls out another cigarette and lights it for her. Jeanne is grateful her friend understands and doesn't press further. She notices her hands are shaking again, like her body is ready to bolt. She would tell Clém to leave him, if the roles were reversed. She'd tell her that she was better off without him. But is that even true at this point?

What about her citizenship and his publishing connections? What about the fact that what little career she has is built on the success of his poetry? She's worried for some time now that Konstantin is like an oxygen machine, and she is a patient hooked up to him, who, without his constant assistance, would die.

She ashes her cigarette onto the sidewalk.

It's just so scary, you know. To lose him. He was my first serious relationship.

Yeah, I suppose that's true. You weren't really into relationships when you were younger, from what I seem to recall.

You can just say I was a slut. Clém smiles ruefully.

No, I can't, because then I'd be calling myself one.

You seem to have calmed down. You're married now.

I mean sure, on paper, but we have an open thing. Simone's idea. I'd never tried an open relationship before, but I really like it.

Oh, that's great. Are either of you seeing anyone else right now? Jeanne asks, enormously relieved that they are off the subject of her marriage.

*

The afternoon continues this way, Jeanne trying to keep the conversation away from Konstantin, quickly swatting away any questions or anything that could relate back to her husband. When Clém looks at her phone and says, I'd better get going, something tugs at Jeanne's heart. She wants to say: *please don't leave me alone here, I don't know what I'm doing or who I'm supposed to be. T'es la seule chose familière dont je me souviens. I don't know if I can face him alone.* Instead, she smiles, thanks her for coming, and kisses her once on each cheek.

Je Me Souviens

Québec's motto, « Je Me Souviens » is relatively recent, replacing the rather boring « La Belle Province » in 1978. It translates as *I remember*, which as mottos go, is fairly mysterious. Remember what? France's loss to the British troops? History, colonisation? A deep love of Québec? According to some, je me souviens was the beginning of a poem that finished: né sous le lys / je croîs sous la rose. Born under the lily, I grow under the rose. The lily stood for France and the rose for England. It always makes Jeanne think of remembering those lost in battle, like the American "Remember the Alamo." But who, exactly, is doing the remembering? And doesn't the directive to remember also imply a forgetting?

She knows how to translate reflexive verbs in French, of course, but a part of her brain stubbornly yields to the English construction, interpreting it as *I remember myself*. She thinks this makes for a more interesting motto. In her mind, Montréal is a magical city, and when you go there, you can recover parts of yourself you lose otherwise. You can remember who you were meant to be, instead of who you are. For her, those three words hold all that possibility.

Remember Jeanne, the city tells her. Remember what, whom? She keeps staring into the universe contained in the cracks of muddy alleyways, holding her breath. Waiting for a signal to materialise. She is a detective now, trying to solve the mystery of her own life. Something tells her she has all the clues she needs already, but the sequence escapes her.

She closes her eyes. What are the true things she can name? She has a body. She is female, with long streaks of male. Her hair is short. She is in Montréal, or Montreal, or else in London, or Paris, or Berlin, or Cleveland. She is stranded somewhere on a violent planet. She is separated or not separated from Konstantin, who she can or cannot trust. She speaks languages, too many languages. She is always overwhelmed, épuisée, at her breaking point.

She is fracturing, breaking infinitely.

She is falling for someone, maybe. She is pinning all her hopes on Mélusine, knowing it's a terrible idea. She should know better. She *does* know better. But she is trying to get away from knowing, from sureness. She doesn't want to be positive or authoritative anymore. She wants the unknown.

So now, instead of bringing her back to herself, the experience of returning to Montréal and seeing Clém once again unleashes a flood of memories within her. And when she finally remembers, it is overwhelming. Some of her memories are beautiful, but others are almost too upsetting to consider, reminding her why she repressed them in the first place.

Jeanne's earliest memory is one of her most unpleasant. There is a toddler still inside her with baby teeth that wants, throwing tantrums, breathless from crying, inconsolable. Her mother at a party smoking a joint, overly drunk and dancing with a man, a not-father. Her real father is elsewhere. Her mother flips the record over as the strange man reaches a lazy hand up mother's skirt.

She is a child sitting in the corner. She has soiled herself. No one is checking her diaper; no one really notices her at all. The child failed by language, unable to express what she wants or needs to others. Who cannot make herself heard, even when she tries to speak. Jeanne has sometimes wondered if this frustration eventually evolved into a lifelong obsession with language. The child tries crying and cries trying for hours, her face blistering red, but they either can't soothe her or don't want to. They stare at her through

186

hash and opium hazes, unsure if she is real. She starts to throw things. She hits her hands against the walls and the floor; she spills her bottle. Elle crie plus fort, plus fort. She screams out her needs to them, and they are horrified. They speak to her in hushed, stern tones, urging her to be quiet, to control herself. They ignore her diaper, until, having exceeded all methods of communication available to her, she is silent, spent with sheer exhaustion.

She can't linger on that memory for too long or she'll start to cry. She closes her eyes again and focuses on recalling her teenage summers in Montréal. These memories are full-colour, vivid, three-dimensional portraits. She can walk around in them. She remembers how anxious Montréalers are for summer after suffering, grumbling through winter every year to no one's surprise. Hands cracked and bloody from frost. Quebeckers have their own special word, frette, that goes beyond froid. It is the coldest cold, colder than cold. They milk as much as they can out of long days and nights in the warm months, knowing the cold will soon come. In the dark, they party hard, then the next day they sprawl out in parks: La Fontaine, Maisonneuve, Baldwin, Jarry. Hangovers hidden beneath a protective layer of sunglasses, reading and sun-stealing. She remembers the simple, effortless beauty of picnics with her friends: caprese salads, shoplifted salami, stone fruits, cheap champagne, fat paperbacks and magazines. She can see ripe peaches resting on blankets in almost pornographic detail, the shining brightness of their insides.

Nuit de la Poésie II

After Clém leaves, Jeanne checks her phone. A message from Mélusine, inviting her to a poetry reading that night at someone's house in Saint-Henri. Jeanne's had enough poetry readings to last her a lifetime, but Mélusine assures her this will be different, more fun, as some friends of hers are reading. In the end, Jeanne's persuaded. She vows not to drink, to be on her best behaviour, and not to make a fool of herself.

The trip takes her twenty minutes on the Métro. She intentionally tries to be a little late, anticipating that she won't know anyone besides Mélusine. Or worse, what if she does? What if her old friends from college are there, and they tell Mélusine about how she ditched them, completely ghosted them for no reason? At this thought, she almost doesn't ring the bell. She's worked so hard to transform herself, she can't afford to backslide.

But in the end, she knows she has to see her again. She would walk on hot coals if that was Mélusine's idea of a date. Her nerves are raw and frayed, but she takes a deep breath and presses the doorbell.

A giggling, feminine voice answers. The kind of voice Jeanne doubts anyone takes too seriously.

Allô!

Hi, I'm here for the poetry reading.

Ahhhh l'amie de Mélusine?

So, she has already been introduced. She can't help but smile a little with pride.

Ouais. Jeanne.

There's another muffled voice over the intercom, and the first voice giggles again, but the words are inaudible to Jeanne. A brief pause, and then someone buzzes her in. She pushes hard on the heavy wooden door and enters the apartment building.

The apartment is 402, so it must be on the 4th floor. She doesn't really need this information, however, because she can already hear laughter and shouts spilling out above her head. There's a joke sign hanging on the door. Instead of ne déranger pas like a hotel it reads, svp déranger. She knocks a few times, but when there is no answer she gets the feeling that the door is open and no one is coming for her. She twists the knob and realises she was correct. As she walks in, she thinks that the poetry reading is like a television with the volume on too high. There are silver balloons everywhere, and she has to be careful to avoid stepping on them. She makes her way into the living room, sliding past good-looking people of all kinds. She is disappointed to see that Mélusine is not among them. Without her, she feels very alone.

Jeanne is very intimidated. Everyone is so art world here, so young, so queer, so fashion. A girl is wearing a white shirt emblazoned in mauve with the words: Lesbian Desert. She stands next to someone with hand tattoos of the male and female symbols, a turquoise mullet, and tiny glasses talking to someone who looks like a new age vampire. They are all drinking ruby-coloured punch.

Jeanne can't find a place to insert herself, and anyway, she doesn't want to talk. Her tongue is swollen, and it's painful to make words come out. She makes her way to the kitchen and thinks she overhears someone say, "I'm exploring making art out of soymilk now." She winces.

She helps herself to a cup of punch, although she doesn't have any idea what's in it and doesn't want to ask. Elle espère qu'elle ne va pas s'évanouir de nouveau et se ridiculiser pas auprès de Mélusine. But nerves get the better of her and she drinks the whole cup of punch fast. And then another. And another. Fear makes her so thirsty.

There's a familiar voice coming from the next room, and she follows it. Mélusine is standing in the doorway wearing a dark purple dress that shows off just enough of her breasts. Tiny stars wink at the sides of her eyes; sequins pasted on with body glue. On most people, it would look childish, but it suits her.

People stand up and acknowledge Mélusine when she arrives. A man slips a drink into her hand, asks her if she wants a bump. She says something and he laughs, puts the baggie away. Jeanne catches her looking around the room, which is when their gazes finally collide. Mélusine winks, throwing her off. Jeanne decides to go eat some chips so that she won't seem needy, to control the urge in her head now, her desire to dance with Mélusine again, to let the rest of the world melt away like a tab of acid on her tongue.

But Mélusine strolls over to her purposefully, unambiguously, and tugs her gently by the collar of her shirt. Jeanne is frightened of what might happen.

You came.

Of course. You thought I wouldn't?

She shrugs, as if she is unaware of her power over people.

I never know what's going on. Anyway, I'm glad you're here. I hope no one's scared you away. My friends can be a bit . . . much.

That's okay, mine too, Jeanne finds herself saying. She smiles, imagining Nat and Mélusine interacting.

Did you get your tongue pierced? Mélusine doesn't miss a thing. Jeanne stares at the floor, embarrassed. Her tongue still hurts, but the punch has taken the edge off.

Yeah, yeah, I did. Today.

God, don't look so dejected! If you're going to have a piercing like that, you have to own it. I think it's great.

Really?

Yes, really. I'm a little jealous.

Her eyes betray something flirtatious that Jeanne tries to ignore. They both stay silent for a few moments, letting it hang over them. It is Mélusine who finally breaks the silence:

How do you feel about the manuscript so far? You can be honest with me.

Oh, I like everything I've gotten to read. A lot.

You don't have to say that.

I know, she says emphatically. I wouldn't be translating it if I didn't connect to or like it, I promise.

Jeanne's telling the truth. When she doesn't care about a book, it shows. The words feel hollow, and the work is painstaking. That's how it was with Konstantin's new poems, drudgework. But spending time with Mélusine's words is a joy, and she feels lucky to have the chance.

Mélusine smiles broadly at her approval, ruby lips parting to reveal a few teeth. In the other room, an outpouring of poetry. They follow the others. There is no space left on the faded burnt sienna couch or any of the chairs, so she and Mélusine sit next to one another on the floor. Jeanne folds her legs pretzel-style, but Mélusine, conscious of her dress, leans her legs to one side.

The person she saw earlier with the glasses and all the tattoos stands up and announces there will be nudity and sex acts. Jeanne is unsure if this is a joke. They start to read a trilingual poem. Spanish, French, English, a kind of ode to hooking up in bathrooms. As they read, a couple also stands up and starts making out. Jeanne can't tell if this is planned. The poet repeats the same words over and over until they transform. It reminds her of that silly Adriano Celetano song that is supposed to imitate American movie speech — "Prisencolinensinainciusol." The way the poet says *écriture* blurs until she hears it in English as: *a creature*. She listens as the words morph again and again.

The poet's next word is *bobettes*, slang for *underwear*, which always sounded more like a French power pop band to Jeanne than anything else: Les Bobettes. The audience is clapping and shouting as the couple slowly peel off their briefs. She can't imagine how Konstantin would respond to this. He would probably call it performance art. She's not even sure if she likes it, but not everything has to be enjoyable. Maybe it can challenge her instead. And her heart is racing — she wants to see it through, she wants to stay close to Mélusine. She knows enough to act nonchalant.

The chants of "bobettes!" multiply and reach a crescendo in the crowd until the couple are naked, save for their socks. But then, instead of fucking, they just hold one another. She watches them embrace, thinking how sweet it is, actually. The poet follows their lead now, reciting gentle lines about the morning after, coming back down to Earth. When they finish, she feels like they've collectively shared something, like the reading belongs to all of them.

There is a short break. Mélusine turns to her.

What did you think of Arturo's work?

She can tell this is a test. She can't compare it to anything, so she chooses her words carefully.

I'm not sure if I liked it, but I was intrigued. It was intense.

Mélusine nods. That's the mot juste. Intense.

Arturo's a friend of yours?

No, we just run in the same circles. I think they're clever, if a bit literal sometimes. The couple that was you know — making out, stripping — they're my friends. Jules and Henri.

The next poet pushes the erotic energy further still. She attempts to read her poem while another woman goes down on her. The poem is about a fig, and Jeanne suddenly understands what Mélusine means by a bit literal. She initially averts her eyes, embarrassed at witnessing their intimacy up close. But she wants to look; everyone else is looking. Eventually, the pull is too strong. In the matter of a few moments she goes from terrified to look to wondering what it would be like to be that woman, exposed and vulnerable in front of strangers. What an incredible turn on it might be. She wonders if anyone will ask for a volunteer.

The poem finishes with what Jeanne strongly suspects is a faked orgasm. Or maybe it's real, who knows, it doesn't sound real to her. Either way, the audience goes wild. Jeanne takes another sip of her punch and registers that she is drunk. Drunk and happy. Any more alcohol, though, and she might black out. She puts her glass down. She wants to remember this.

Night dips lower, and Mélusine introduces her to more of her friends. Jeanne starts to sweat a little, still intimidated. Jules is the rare one, born and raised in Montréal. He is a bartender who writes short stories in his spare time. His mostly buzzed hair is bleached blond, and he is wearing a shirt that says Refus Global. She doesn't expect much from his stories; everyone says that they're a writer these days, but when he reads from his work, she perks up. His writing is observant and blisteringly angry.

She spends most of her time talking with Jules' partner, Henri. It is as if he and Jules assessed their attractiveness levels and concluded that they were perfectly even and decided to date. Henri is a film-maker, although when she asks what his work is about he begins a long, meandering explanation involving terms like *new queer cinema*, *experimental*, and *cinema verité*. The silver earring dangling from his ear shimmers as he speaks. Jeanne can't take her eyes off it.

What is it really about though? Like what happens in the story?

I mean, more or less, it's essentially footage of me and Jules having sex. Set to a bangin' soundtrack.

Oh. Well, I'd watch that. He grins.

I like you, Jeanne. You're alright. So what do you do? God, that's such a boring question. But I'm curious.

I'm a literary translator.

No shit? What do you translate?

In the past, mostly poetry. From Russian or French into English. Right now I'm actually working on something with Mélusine, though.

You lucky bitch! She never shows us any of her writing. She's secretive, that one. Holds her cards close to the chest.

What are you all talking about? Mélusine interrupts. She winks at Jeanne.

Is Henri bullying you?

No, quite the opposite. I'm charmed by your new friend.

Jeanne's a gem, isn't she?

Quite. Where are you from again?

She thinks about it. She is having trouble remembering the answer, but it's on the tip of her tongue. Montréal? Or was it London. Or the United States? But what state, what state? Should she answer as Jean, Jeanne, or John? Does the question *where are you from* refer to the place she was born, the place she grew up, the place she identifies most with, or the place she currently lives?

Henri cuts her off, answering his own query.

I know everyone hates that question anyway, *I* hate it. I'm not even sure why I asked. Sorry, he says.

Jeanne is not used to this feeling of being accepted, even appreciated, at a poetry reading. Every conversation does not feel like a trap designed to test her intelligence, to trick her into saying something stupid or to put her work as a translator down. No one is involved in a pissing contest or trying to quietly destroy someone else. There are far fewer men than at Konstantin's readings, she realises, and it seems that no one here is straight. Including her.

She realises that she's not surrounded by strangers anymore. Everyone keeps offering her their phone numbers. She switches from English to French easily, sometimes merging the two as Franglais, the booze loosening her tongue and with it, her self-consciousness. No one here will be upset if she says *marde* instead of *merde*; in fact, it might be preferable. Mélusine's friends, at least on the surface, don't favour one language over another; they speak many languages between them. She catches strands of Arabic, Spanish, Haitian Creole. No one here is interested in whether or not their language is the "correct" version; they're too busy disregarding the rules, inventing their own alphabets, dreaming up neologisms, playing. Jeanne leans her head down on a pillow, watching everyone chat and dance around her, drowsy and content.

De/pêché

They crawl up the last steps to Mélusine's apartment. They are ben drunk. Jeanne grins when she inhales the familiar scent of Papier D'Arménie. The smell tells her she's returned to a kind of home. It tells her she is in the right place. Jeanne remembers Konstantin for a fleeting second, but he feels so far away, he may as well be at the bottom of the sea.

Jeanne spots Mélusine's black chair and gets an idea.

Wait here, she tells Mélusine, who smiles with delight. Some kind of game, her favourite.

Jeanne wants to be in control. She sits down in the chair, legs open like a man's. She tries to appear cool and collected, though inside every cell screams. She fixes her face so that it is emotionless. She needs to be convincing.

Stay there, but let me look at you, she says.

Mélusine looks bashful. Then she smirks as if to say: *here I am.*

Ôte ta robe, Jeanne instructs.

Mélusine stares at her, surprised by her forwardness. Silently, she obeys. Lifts the slip dress over her head. Underneath, a black lace bra and matching panties. So delicate they could disintegrate between her fingertips. Jeanne drinks her in with wonder but quickly represses it. She can't care, she can't show anything if this is going to work.

Good. Now come here and give me a lap dance. Jeanne hears the words outside herself, as if someone else is speaking through her. She is never commanding, never sure of what she wants. She is used to being on the other end, taking it. Even last time with Violette, she let someone else lead. But not tonight.

Mélusine obeys again but not before making a slight adjustment. She goes to the record player, puts on something haunting and old. *Musique diabolique*, Jeanne thinks. Then she makes her way towards Jeanne. She turns around, hiding her face. Jeanne feels the slender body brush against her jeans and t-shirt. She just barely senses the outline of lingerie against the denim. If she had a cock, it would be rock hard right now. She still can't see Mélusine's face. It drives her crazy. She reaches a hand out to touch her, and it is immediately slapped away, hard.

Still facing away from Jeanne, Mélusine takes one hand and unhooks her bra, tossing it against the wall. Jeanne feels a jolt run through her, the anticipation unbearable. She throbs between her legs and fears she will break character. *Not yet*, she tells herself.

Mélusine turns around now, raises herself to full height. Jeanne can see her breasts, dark shadows crossing her chest. She senses the power shift and cedes it happily. Mélusine sits down in her lap, so that they are finally face to face. There is a terrifying hunger in her eyes that matches her own, and she knows there is no going back now.

And then she is whispering into Mélusine's neck, nuzzling, staining skin with her breath. She kisses the lion tattoo on her shoulder, then lifts her hands up and places them gently on Mélusine's breasts. This time, she doesn't slap them away. Their mouths a soft collision, careful dance and calibration until they find the sweet spot. Jeanne's piercing adds a new sensation: a cold, metallic pearl buried in the warmth.

Jeanne aches at the kiss. She has the bizarre sentiment of still wanting Mélusine, even when she has her. She gently steers her towards the couch, where she lays her down on the throw pillows. Tugs her underwear free. Mélusine gives her a knowing look she can't decipher. She's stripped of all her pretences, façades gone. Seulement reste le désir. Jeanne brings her mouth in close again. Then it's a blur. Like this:

Air in, air out. Licking, lungs full of M. Strands of black hair cling to lips. *You want it rough?* Proud, boasting. *How badly do you want it?* A look that says: *do your worst. Ok. As you wish.* Grasping a knot of hair, an anchor. Twists. Pulls hard. A sharp cry. Shock, *Ouch!* pain blooms. *What, you didn't think I'd hurt you?* Almost angry, but soon M. thaws into a soft syrup. *Good girl.* Warm, faint murmurs, skin touching skin. Thrill. Prickling anticipation. *Don't stop.* M. lays back into cushion. Brutal passion. A flood; it's too much. *Oh my god. Oh my fucking god. I'm going to . . .*

A short wait, a blunt look. Wild, hungry abandon. Pink blush mouthing: *again, again.* Mouthing: *I want.* Want what? *I want you.*

*

And then it hits Jeanne, what she's been missing. What Mélusine means to her:

ecstasy   euphorie   excitement

     reverie

           hedonism

             émotion

       sensuality

révolte   insouciance

debauchery

espièglerie

liberté

everything.

*

Afterwards, she is finally allowed to sleep in Mélusine's bedroom. She enters with quiet reverence, as if going to church. They dive under the sheets, naturally folding into one another. Mélusine's head is pressed against her bare chest, and she strokes her dark hair in disbelief.

In the morning, Mélusine is once again gone before she wakes up, and Jeanne is a little disappointed. She'd imagined them curled together in the bed, gentle morning sex, getting coffee together afterwards, walking around the neighbourhood and reading the paper. There is a note, promising to contact her later, signed "un gros bec," a huge kiss. She takes this as a positive sign. No crêpes this time, only a cold coffee that she reheats in a pot on the stovetop because there is no microwave. The message is clear: *don't get too comfortable, don't expect special treatment every time.* Which is fine with Jeanne. She still can't even believe they slept together, the noises that came out of her mouth.

Remembering why she's here, she returns to Mélusine's manuscript. She reads it through once again, marking down any words that come up multiple times. Words that turn up frequently, Jeanne finds, are important to the author, whether consciously or unconsciously. Signposts, useful for figuring out the themes and heart of a piece of writing, as well as determining the work's internal rhythm and sound (in order to preserve that rhythm and sound in a completely different language). She reads some of the passages out loud to herself, quietly.

Around noon, she starts to feel weird staying in Mélusine's place all alone. She heads out, locking the door behind her.

She walks past the Village, the drag queen bars and sex shops where she used to buy poppers. Then she passes Parc La Fontaine, self-righteous runners racing through the wide path framed on either side by trees, the placid blue-green lake imprisoned by endless summer construction. She spots a woman walking her cat on a leash and smiles.

Soon, without realising, she enters the hubbub of the Plateau. The streets are mostly blocked off so that people can stroll and hopefully shop, uninterrupted. The tourists are easy to spot, especially the Americans. They are yelling, and they can't stop saying how much Montréal reminds them of Paris.

She feels tired, overwhelmed by the crowds. She ducks into a side street off Mont-Royal where she knows she will find a variety of bookstores, English and French. With the first few shops, she is content to léche-vitrine at all the new titles, but by the third, she gets curious and goes in to take a peek.

She walks into a new and used bookstore with titles in several languages. The poetry section is in the back left corner, taunting her. She avoids it like the plague, because what if. What if he is there, lurking. But finally, when she has looked at every other part of the store, including the birthday cards, she decides to at least give it a glance. They probably don't have Konstantin's book, right? This is a small independent bookstore; they're bound to be missing a few titles. She scans the shelf for his last name, a last name that should be hers, a last name she immediately rejected. And then she sees it. They have one copy of *Exile* under staff recommendations.

She picks up his book carefully, flipping to the back where a black-and-white author photo shows him looking smug, cold, and handsome. Serious, a real poet. She remembers when the photos were taken, and he was furious they had not Photoshopped out the birthmark on his left cheek. He usually tried hard to angle it away in photos, although it was smaller than the size of a quarter and no one cared besides him. The biography does not mention that he is married to his translator, only that he was born in Saint Petersburg and currently lives in London. She wonders how many women have read this exact biography and assumed that he was single. How many people assumed his book spontaneously translated itself. She wonders if he had anything to do with the sparseness of the paragraph. She fixates on his transgressions and her invisibility until she begins to get very, very angry.

Sans avertissement, une rage se construit et se construit jusqu'à ce qu'elle la saisisse, bloquant tout le reste. Pressure splits her head like a migraine. Слепая ярость. She thinks: *I have to do something.* She surveys the room to make sure no one is looking, then pulls out a black Sharpie from her jacket. On the cover, right on top of Konstantin's name, she scrawls *TRANSLATED BY JEANNE ARSENAULT.* She stabs the sharpie in as she forms the letters, black ink corroding the cardstock. Her name is now much larger than his, the main text visible on the cover. As she does this, a weight is released, the cranial pressure starts to dissipate.

Madame.

Behind her, the bookstore owner appears, frowning. Madame, on ne peut pas défigurer les livres. Veuillez payer pour ça, he says.

Oh, I've paid for it, let me assure you, she replies. The joke is lost on him. He continues to frown, offended. She feels out of control, the candied rush of adrenaline. Anything is possible now.

Her instinct is to run away clutching the book, but she reminds herself that the point is recognition, not shoplifting. With an insane smile, she calmly places the book back on the shelf and dashes out of the store. The owner follows after her yelling:

Madame! Vous devez payer! Voleuse!

*

Her legs don't stop running until she reaches the Métro station, where without even thinking she hops on the first train that comes and somehow ends up in Hochelaga. Then she collapses on a bus-stop bench, breathing heavily. Alone, she laughs like a lunatic, harder and harder. She feels like an outlaw, someone her younger self would be proud of. She can't wait to tell Mélusine what she's done. She knows it's the kind of thing she will appreciate. Part of her is a little ashamed — it feels so childish, petty revenge in place of real power. But it's just the first step of something bigger. She buys herself an ice cream cone to celebrate her liberation and eats it messily as she walks. Milk swirled with sweet berry juice drips onto the sidewalk. Frozen tongue, faint strawberry numb. She loves the taste, but it's too much sugar, especially after all the punch she drank the night before. Her body rejects it. She finds an alley to vomit in, and a mother walking by with two children shoots her a look of disgust and pulls her children quickly away.

Once she composes herself, she stops at a public library to charge her phone and starts to work on Mélusine's translation again. Now that her insides are clear, she feels better. Her mind is buzzing, alert. Devouring the manuscript. In her writing, she notices Mélusine ignores grammar and punctuation, making her sentences cascade and crash like a waterfall. Jeanne is beginning to put together a skeleton of the work, then slowly filling it out with skin, figuring out the curves and muscles. When she can eat and breathe the text, when it moves within her body like it is her own, then she will know that she truly understands it. The structure of Mélusine's writing will not be easy to preserve, and the fact that it will mirror her own translation on every page makes it even more intimidating. But that's the challenge, what draws her to it.

A violet light flashes as her phone comes back to life. Mélusine has not texted or called. She's a little disappointed, although she's not sure what she expected — something about how great last night was? Praise for her sexual abilities? As she feared, however, there are many messages from Konstantin. He hasn't tried to call again, probably because it is too expensive. She learns that, after some delays, he has finally made it back to London, and is going to check on the flat and to repack his belongings. Once he's done, he will catch a nonstop flight to Montréal.

> A red eye. With customs,
> should arrive tmrw around 1pm.

Intellectually, Jeanne knows what red eye means of course, but she can't get the image of his eyes piercing the dark bloody red out of her head. She can feel his urgency in the texts, his frustration that he can't grab her by the wrist. He can't reach across time and space, but that's exactly what he wants. Maybe his flight will be delayed or cancelled, but even so, her time alone is running out. She has one more day. Whatever she has to say to Mélusine, she needs to say it now. She texts her first:

> Can we meet tonight?

Mélusine texts her back a few minutes later:

> No, not tonight.

Knots harden in Jeanne's stomach. But it has to be tonight. She can't hold him off much longer.

> K is coming tomorrow.

I have to meet him.
Plz can we talk
for a few minutes?

Maybe. I'll see what i can do.

She feels pathetic but sighs a little shiver of relief. It's something. She knows she's being needy, a pest, but she's also confident Mélusine will understand.

Only when she's talked to Mélusine does she text Konstantin.

Sorry! My phone died.

He replies right away. She pictures him waiting by his phone in their flat, or is it his flat again now? Part of her just wants to forfeit all her belongings and to give them to him, anything to get away, a clean slate.

Thats OK.
I was just worried about you.
I almost called the police but
I wasnt even sure who to call
or what to say

She knows he's exaggerating. He would never have called the police, he doesn't believe in that sort of thing. But she recognizes the way she is handling this, by trying to avoid him forever, is immature. Maybe he is genuinely concerned. He's abandoning punctuation in his texts in a way she has not seen before. He adds:

> I didnt hear from you
> and there were bizarre
> charges on my credit cards
> and I thought maybe
> youd been kidnapped.
> I know thats crazy but
> I was just so worried.

Ah, there it is. He's noticed the credit card charges. He must know it's her and want her to know that he knows. The purchases, though, are not things he would normally associate with her. Video gambling, X-rated films. She decides to leave his comment hanging there, unaddressed.

> Really, I'm fine.

> I've just been so busy working
> on this translation project and
> I don't know…
> being back in mtl is weird.
> A lot of ghosts to contend with.

> wait what translation project?

Oh, the one I came here for.
That woman I told you about?

You accepted it?
What about my book?
youre under contract.

Even though it's just a text, she can hear his voice: *I own you. I still own you.*

I can handle two projects at once.
Don't worry.

But you didn't even talk to me
before you accepted.
youre my translator.

I don't need your permission.

She can feel the blood rushing to her head, her breath quickening. How fucking dare he. He can't control her.

He doesn't respond after that. He must be in transit or not have service. She doesn't ever want Thursday to come.

She gets impatient waiting for Mélusine to respond to her about whether or not they can meet. In the end, she decides to just go to Mélusine's apartment. She's memorised the address. She knows it's not polite to turn up uninvited, but everything feels so pressing with the threat of Konstantin and his red eyes coming tomorrow. His arrival feels like the end of the world.

But she tells herself to prepare to find something she doesn't want to see. If Mélusine has another lover over, she thinks she can handle it. She can't see how it would take anything away from what the two of them share. They aren't even dating, and she doesn't want to marry her, after all. No, all she wants from Mélusine is to collaborate, to share in art-making. And she wants to tell her how she feels about her. She doesn't want to hold it inside anymore.

When she gets to Mélusine's apartment, she notices that the front door is slightly ajar. *What if Mélusine's hurt, someone's broken in and attacked her? What if she's in there, bleeding on the floor?* A current of fear shoots through Jeanne as she imagines that Konstantin has found her and tried to exact some sort of revenge. Deep down, she knows this isn't what's going on, but it gives her just enough of an excuse. She announces herself loudly, then pushes on the door.

Silence. She walks through the apartment, noticing papers all over the floor, books pulled off the bookshelf and strewn everywhere. She keeps calling Mélusine's name as she heads towards the bedroom, afraid of what she might find. When she enters her room and no one is there, she starts to panic. But then she hears a trail of soft little noises coming from behind the locked door. Only, the door isn't locked this time. Like the front door, it's slightly ajar, light pouring out of it. She takes this as an invitation. She cracks it open, peeks inside.

In the centre of the room, there is a child wearing blue overalls covered in paint marks. He is playing with some plastic toy cars, making them smash into each other over and over. He makes explosion noises, then drops the cars, watching them clatter on the carpet with delight. When he hears the door squeak open, he stops and turns to Jeanne with wide eyes.

He looks to be about six or seven. His hair falls in dark black curls, and his eyes are a warm amber. He is not afraid of her. After a moment, he smiles, perhaps an invitation to play. Then, he sticks his tongue out at her. Jeanne can't help but laugh.

Hi, Jeanne says.

Hi, the boy echoes. What is your name?

John, she tells him, just to see what will happen. He accepts this, no resistance.

Hi John. Do you have any cookies?

She laughs again and shakes her head no. Are those your cars? She points to his toys.

Yeah, I make them crash, go sploooosh. But don't be scared. It's not real.

Jeanne is touched by how seriously he says this, concerned that she is caught up in his game and wanting to reassure her.

She is about to sit down and to play with him when she hears a gasp behind her.

She watches as the blood drains from Mélusine's face, looking between Jeanne and the boy. Is this her secret? Jeanne wonders. She's kidnapped a child? She's trafficking children? She's a part-time babysitter? She knows none of these are it but can't quite put the puzzle together.

Mélusine is speaking to the boy in rushed French, words that sound like they are on fire. He abandons his cars and retreats to a corner of the room. She turns to Jeanne.

You have to leave now. You shouldn't have come inside.

I knocked. I called out for you.

You can't just go walking into any room like you live here.

The door was open. I got worried.

I was just taking out the trash, I was coming right back.

Ok, I'm sorry I came in uninvited. But can you just tell me what's going on? Who is the kid?

Mélusine looks down at the floor, then at the boy, then finally at Jeanne.

You can't tell anyone, Jeanne. Swear.

Jeanne swears immediately. She has to know. Nothing is adding up.

Mélusine gestures to the boy.

This is my son. His name is Léo.

Oh. OH.

*

Of all the responses Jeanne expects, this is not among them. But now that she reflects back, it's painfully obvious. She sees that the room is decorated like a child's room. There is a bookshelf of kids' books, neat little translucent boxes full of toys and clothes in the chest of drawers. Everything starts to click. The books and papers scattered all over her floor. The snacks in the fridge. Her lion tattoo. The stuffed elephant. He even looks like her, in the eyes especially.

She tries to do the maths. If he's six now, she had him when she was seventeen or eighteen? She would've been almost a child herself. But when did she do this? And with whom?

This must come as a shock to you.

It does, but Jeanne doesn't say that.

No, no I get it. You don't owe me anything. You have every right to keep this private.

There's a very specific reason I keep this private. It has nothing to do with you. I keep this from everyone.

Jeanne shrugs. Still, that's your prerogative. It's very personal.

Mélusine's expression darkens.

215

I don't want to do this anymore. I'll tell you everything, but it's not a happy story. And you must promise me not to repeat a word to anyone. This is a life and death matter, I'm serious.

Jeanne solemnly nods, intrigued.

She says something else to Léo, then closes the door softly behind them, leaving him to play alone.

Mélusine leads Jeanne into the living room, and they sit on the same couch where they fucked the night before. Mélusine picks up a teacup and takes a sip, and Jeanne notices her hands shaking.

I knew I'd have to come clean to you about this at some point. It's not that I want to hide him, obviously. Léo is everything to me. This was for his safety.

Jeanne says nothing, waiting for her to continue. She does not want to interfere with her getting the words out.

My real name is not Mélusine. It's a pseudonym. When I moved to Montréal, I started over. I wanted to create a new persona, this young, glamorous artist with no past. I'm sure you can understand.

Jeanne can understand just as well as if it were her speaking these words. She listens intently.

I was born in Paris. My mother is Algerian, my father is French. When I was young, I fell in love with a very dangerous man. A violent man. He got me pregnant, I think to trap me. I didn't know I was pregnant for a long time because I kept losing weight, and I thought the missed period was just stress because it had happened to me before. Things were so bad between us, I feared for my life. He tried to strangle me while I was pregnant. Then he pushed me down a flight of stairs in our apartment because he thought I was cheating on him. That was the last straw. I went to the doctor, and when I came back, I sobbed and told him there was no heartbeat. There was, but I was so scared for us, I cried and cried. I really thought I would lose my baby.

Jeanne has the urge to put her hand on Mélusine's shoulder and comfort her, but does not. Instead she looks into her eyes, face trained in concentration.

I knew I had to leave in secret, but I didn't have anywhere to go. My sister, Soraya, was in the process of moving to Canada because she was engaged to a Canadian man, but my ex didn't know that. I escaped with the help of my family. They told him I disappeared. I guess he bought it. He didn't seem to care much after he thought the baby was gone. Or maybe he left the country too, I don't know. My sister got me a place to stay.

Mélusine pauses to look out the window, as if she expects to see her ex's face there. She stirs almond milk into her tea longer than necessary, continuing to swirl her teaspoon in tight circles long after the milk is integrated. Through gritted teeth, she continues:

I immediately started using a different name, and I don't let any outlets publish photos of me, only my work. It's dangerous being an artist because he could find me, in theory. So only my closest friends know about my son. I am very careful to keep him hidden so that word doesn't get back to Paris. And to be honest, I'm cautious about who I introduce to Léo anyway. I have to be sure someone is going to stick around for good and that they are looking out for our best interests.

I know I can't do it forever. When he gets older, it will be harder. I'll tell him more when he's ready to understand, and he can make his own decisions about whether or not he wants to meet his father. I could've done it through the proper channels. Gone to court, filed a restraining order. But sometimes none of that works. The women's shelter I stayed at, they told me it usually escalates in severity. If he'd already pushed me down the stairs, who knew what else he was capable of? I had to do this to save both of us.

Mélusine says this as though she is in court, trying to plead her case. A jagged thought lodges itself in the back of Jeanne's mind: what if she had gotten pregnant with Konstantin's child? What if she was tied to him like that, forever? She shudders. She probably would've done the same thing as Mélusine if put in the same situation; fled in the night. Alors, en réalité, elle ne garderait pas l'enfant.

Another thought she can barely admit: she is not completely sure Mélusine is telling her the truth right now. She wants to trust her, in many ways it feels gross to even question the story, like a man who asks *What she was wearing?* But the fact is that they don't know each other that well, and it seems that Mélusine has already kept things from her. Maybe she is not a good judge of character at all. But she tries to quell these fears, says nothing, waits to hear her out.

She continues: My sister and her husband watch Léo a few days a week. He goes to the same school as their daughter, his cousin Nour. So they'll pick them up together, and they'll have a sleepover and then take them to school or camp in the morning, or sometimes I'll take him out for breakfast and then bring him over myself. And then some days I'll take Léo and Nour for a night, but usually not as often, because I'm only one person and they're a lot to handle.

She smiles, and Jeanne knows she doesn't mean this unkindly. Her love for her son is the clearest thing about her.

Our system works pretty well until days like today, when it doesn't, when it all crumbles. Listen, Jeanne — everything I've said about how I feel about you, about working together — I meant it. And I'll give you honesty, all the honesty you can take from here on out.

They exchange a look and Jeanne thinks: *I really hope you mean it.*

You're playing with fire, publishing this book, Jeanne says. The art world is very small.

219

She doesn't mean to say it aloud; it slips out. It's a terrible business strategy, to discourage her client from publishing, but this is bigger than her. Mélusine is being reckless. How long before someone photographs her, and it ends up on the internet? How long before something about her son gets back to this dangerous man?

But looking at Mélusine's face, she can tell that carrying this secret for so long has worn her out. Maybe part of her wants to be done with it all.

She'd sensed that Mélusine was testing her, and now she knows why. The reason is far less sinister than anything she'd come up with, which gives her some relief.

And yet, her whole relationship with Mélusine suddenly feels more urgent. What are they doing? Has she broken all the rules? Are they dating? Is it serious, is it going anywhere? She doesn't think she can be a mother to a little boy, no matter how cute and rakish. But is Mélusine even expecting that of her?

She doesn't say any of this now. Now is not the right time. They embrace. Mélusine is crying. Jeanne holds her until she stops crying and dries her tears. Then the two of them play a game of hide and seek with her son until it is time for bed.

*

Morning hits her hard.

He's here. She can sense it in the air. Reluctantly, she checks her phone. Konstantin has already texted several times.

Where are you?

Jean where are you.

Jean I'm serious,
I'm going to use the
tracking on your phone
and come to you
if you don't meet me
somewhere.

OK. Have it your way.

He has had an entire conversation with her before she's even woken up. It makes her want to see him even less. She knows he will be angry. She's postponed it for days and fucked two people in the interim. But she owes him this conversation at least. And she's worried he won't take no for an answer.

*

She texts him:

Heading to a café.
I'll message you the address.

Public is better, she thinks. The more people around, the safer she will be.

She goes back to the hotel to shower and to change clothes. As she's showering, she gets an idea. She rifles around in her suitcase and retrieves the green notebook, Konstantin's notebook, setting it out on the hotel desk. The notebook looks like it's been through hell, battered and bent. She's never allowed herself to look inside before, but the pages are yellowed and covered in blue ink, a strange shade she doesn't recognise. Something they only sell in Russia. The script is heavy, huge imprints, some lines violently crossed out at least four times, as if to ensure no one ever sees them. There are ink smudges and fingerprints throughout, and rough edges where pages have been torn out. She's puzzled; the pages are filled with many of the poems she recognises, poems that Konstantin published. But they are not in his handwriting.

She knows his handwriting well, maybe even better than her own. She's seen his signature on hundreds of receipts. In the front of the notebook it reads: Property of Yuri Sokolov. His friend? Or is this a different Yuri? Well, if it's the Yuri she's heard of, she thinks, nothing strange there. So Konstantin's friend wrote down some of his poems, and he kept the notebook as a memory. Maybe Konstantin was working on them, thinking aloud, and Yuri was acting as a scribe.

The problem is that the poems are dated; the first one is from 2005. At least a decade before Konstantin ever published anything. And there are notes for all the poems, drafts, edits, reworkings. She can trace the trains of thought that led to each poem, and they are connected to Yuri's life, not Konstantin's grandparents or his past like he said. Her eyes unfocus; she struggles to understand what she is looking at, what this might mean. This looks bad. Like these are not Konstantin's poems. They never were.

Perhaps the notebook is fake, she thinks, some kind of bizarre prank he is playing on her. Or maybe Konstantin did it to comfort himself in his grief, some strange way of communicating with Yuri. Or there is a third person involved. Or maybe this is some sort of red herring meant to distract her, to divert her attention away from something worse. She has no idea.

No, that's not true. Deep down, she has a theory. A theory that would explain why his new poems were so different, so bad in comparison to the earlier ones. Her gut tells her she has already found the answer. His reaction will confirm it. *I've got you*, she thinks. *Sick bastard. Liar. I've got you at last.*

*

She changes her mind and decides to meet him at the Gibeau Orange Julep instead of a café. Orange Julius, written in Canadian French. She had only been there as a child and remembers the top of the bright orange sphere covered in snow and ice. There's a rumour that the original owner, Hermes Gibeau, lived in the top of the orange with his family. A fucked up Québec fairytale, raising a family inside a fruit, feeding your children sugar crystals every day. She likes how it looks so ridiculous, unbearably giant and garish sitting without explanation next to the highway. More importantly, she knows Konstantin will be disgusted by the exterior. It goes against all of his aesthetics. Too loud, impossible not to spot. She sees the building from blocks away, the scene unfolding like something out of a dream: the day-glo orange sphere, like a sunset melting into the pavement. Liquid happiness, "fait de jus d'orange Sunkist."

She gets there first, but doesn't order anything. She's sweating. The air smells of exhaust. Most of the other people in line are children and parents, looking at her a little perplexed. She smiles at them and shrugs.

After a few minutes, Konstantin walks up, wild-eyed, looking lost. He hasn't slept, she thinks. He doesn't order anything, just searches for her and hurries over as soon as he spots her. Она смотрит в сторону. In what she hopes is a neutral tone, she greets him, and asks how his flight was, how he is settling into the hotel.

почему у тебя такое лицо?

He's looking at her like she's crazy, and she doesn't realise anything is wrong until he says,

Why do you keep speaking Russian?

What? I am? I didn't realise it.

Writing in Russian, speaking in Russian . . . Why is it slipping past her notice all of a sudden? Or is he lying, just trying to fuck with her?

He reaches a hand towards her and she pulls away. He grimaces.

What the hell is in your hair?

She reaches a hand up to check her scalp. Glitter, she says, smiling. No doubt from Mélusine. Is she speaking in Russian now, or French? No. Definitely English. It sticks to her gums.

And do, do you have a — you got your tongue pierced, Jean?

She'd nearly forgotten about it. She can't help but smile now; a bad teen caught in the act. She sticks it out for him to see.

And your shirt's on backwards. But mainly, it's the tongue that concerns me.

Do you like it?

He shakes his head. You look ridiculous. You're not fifteen years old anymore. I'm starting to wonder if you need psychiatric help.

It's called fun, Konstantin. It wouldn't kill you to have some now and then.

He rolls his eyes, like this doesn't deserve a response. But he decides to leave the issue of the tongue piercing alone for the moment.

Where were you this morning? It took you forever to respond to my text.

Un autre monde, she thinks. Un autre monde loin du tien, que je déteste. She doesn't say this though.

I was with Mélusine. Going over the translation.

You should've just come to my hotel once I texted you.

I told you I came here for work, Konstantin.

You could've told her it was important and met me sooner.

But I didn't want to, she thinks. *I didn't want to, that's enough of a reason.*

If you cared about me, you would've come to see me after I flew here, just to be with you. Clearly, only one of us is in this marriage. I give you so much, Jean, and you don't do anything. You treat me like shit.

He is always cramming more words into her mouth before she even has a chance to gather her thoughts. She knows he wants to get a rise out of her, to hurt her as much as possible, but for once, she has the upper hand. He's in a country that's not his own, and she has Mélusine, who makes anything feel possible. Even the possibility that it might not be too late for happiness.

He sighs. Do you want anything he says, I'm going to get a drink.

Sure. A julep and a burger.

An orange julep?

Yeah, the only kind they have.

He nods and gets in the line. The orange juleps attract dozens of wasps to the area, and they're making him fidgety, nervous. She enjoys seeing him sweat. When he catches her watching she looks away, starts playing with her phone. She texts Nat and Layla to let them know she is ok and in Montréal but doesn't elaborate.

He is gone for a long time but eventually comes back with the promised julep and burger. She thanks him, thinking that her choice of location was good. If he was going to hurt her, he would not do it here.

She sips her orange julep slowly. More cream and sugar than she remembers. Dairy was added to the recipe to save on expensive orange juice, to thin it out. And there's an acrid aftertaste, almost chemical. She can't place it.

The truth is, I haven't felt like myself since I got here. I don't feel like myself much these days. Montréal is doing something to me.

Yes, I can see that. You're entitled, that's what it is. You think everything has to revolve around you.

No, I'm just — she stops. There's a sharp, stabbing pain in her stomach. It feels like her insides are collapsing. Something is wrong. She's heard of appendixes bursting and assuming that is maybe what is happening. Something large has burst within her, and the pain radiates all over.

She takes another sip of the julep, because it's the closest thing to water available. She should ask for a ginger ale.

Are you ok? He sees her clutching one hand to her stomach and grimacing with pain. She can't hide it.

No, something's wrong. The pain returns, more aggressive than before. She moans. I don't know what's going on, she cries.

But as soon as she voices it out loud, she does. The julep, the strange aftertaste, the glint in his eyes. He wouldn't. There's no way. Would he?

She can barely speak now because of the pain, but she starts:

Did you . . .?

What she hears him say is:

Listen, Jean, I had to. You have to die so I can live. He says it calmly, but there is fear in his eyes.

She puts it all together seconds too late.

The drink slips out of her hand as her mind slips. Out of her body as her. Body comes crashing. Down creamsicle liquid floods the street. Everything goes. Black, and there are no more words.

*

Jeanne wakes up in the hospital. She thinks she is alive. She doesn't remember how she got here, only that she is supposed to be dead. There is too much light.

Konstantin sits beside her in a chair. He looks genuinely concerned. She glares at him, emboldened for once. Fuming.

Jean. I'm so glad you're ok.

Her throat is completely dry, and her voice comes out hoarse, rusty water from a spout.

You told me I had to die so that you could live!

I did not. Jean, calm down. You were sick, hallucinating.

You poisoned me!

I would never do that.

Then why am I in the hospital? Why did my insides collapse?

I — I'm sorry. The truth is, I did put some vodka in the julep, because I was so nervous. I meant to put it in mine. I guess I gave you the wrong one by mistake.

She looks in his eyes to see if he is telling the truth.

I was scared. You seemed different. I was afraid you would try to divorce me.

His fear and sadness seem authentic, but she can't be sure. After realising he stole Yuri's poems, she doesn't trust a word that comes out of his mouth. Anything could be a play, a manipulation.

You didn't poison me?

No, they said that you fainted. You've barely been eating, you've been drinking constantly. You're completely dehydrated. The doctors said you don't have enough electrolytes or potassium.

Jeanne considers this, still suspicious of everything he says. She tries to remember the last time she ate something. A few bites of sandwich with Clém, crêpes, an ice cream cone. But how long ago . . . one, two, three days? She's eaten little and thrown up most of what she's managed to get down. There's not much in her besides cigarette tar and orange vodka slush.

You need rest. I'm going to take care of you.

She's weak, but manages to shake her head in a defiant NO. He will not be doing any such thing, of that she is certain. She wants Mélusine but does not want to even say her name in front of Konstantin. She asks for her phone, and he looks surprised, hands it to her.

I'm fine, really. You can go now.

Jean. I can't leave you like this.

You've left me in worse states.

What's that supposed to mean?

She does her best attempt at a yell, but it is still a barely raised voice. She wants to mention his infidelity, the chlamydia, but it doesn't even seem relevant anymore. It's not really what she's upset about.

You abused me, Konstantin. You hurt me psychologically and physically.

He looks wildly around to see if anyone is listening.

Get out of here. We can talk when I'm better.

But Jean —

I'm serious. Get the fuck out, Konstantin. I don't want you here. I'm going to call the nurse if you don't leave.

He takes his time but eventually leaves, looking wounded.

As soon as he's gone, Jeanne feels relief, like she's removed a shard of glass from her leg. But he will almost certainly be back. She knows this isn't the end. She reaches for her phone. Her head aches, and her vision is blurry; she manages to text Mélusine the location of the hospital and her room number before she passes out once again.

Cauchemar

Jeanne sleeps badly.

She dreams she is lost in the Black Forest, that dense forest of language Benjamin wrote about, and something is chasing her. A grey wolf, tracking her female scent. His howl makes her quiver with fear. He closes in, salivating. She can see him behind her racing through the fog, red I's trained on her body. She yells for help, but there is no one around for miles, just anonymous trees. No matter how hard she tries to run, he just keeps getting closer. She can't push her legs harder than they are already going. She is growing tired. He notices and increases his pace until he is inches behind, jaws snapping at her, slashing her clothing. She screams. He keeps coming, relentless, even faster now. One final burst of speed, a jump, and then he is on her, tearing her body apart one piece at a time, deconstructing her with rabid pleasure. His teeth sink into her face, biting her flesh and ripping it off. Foam flies all over as he eats. He mangles the skin from her face until she is unrecognisable. Only her two eyes remain, staring out vacantly in a sea of blood. Then, sated, he leaves her. Bleeding and faceless in the woods. Ce n'est plus une personne. She could be anyone, anyone at all.

*

Jeanne screams. Her eyelids flutter open.

Her head is lying in Mélusine's lap.

Am I dead? she asks sincerely, looking up into her eyes.

Mélusine laughs nervously.

I hope not! You just passed out hard. You were snoring so loudly, I didn't want to wake you.

No, no. I'm dead. That's what happened. He poisoned me. Or he made me black out on purpose, or something.

She hears her own voice as she says it, but it sounds far away, faint.

Who poisoned you?

Konstantin.

Mélusine gives her a measured look. She's not looking at Jeanne like she's crazy, but she's looking at her as if deciding whether or not she is crazy.

Why would he do that?

Because I'm leaving him, and he's angry.

Well, let him be angry then. He sounds like a real connard.

He's dangerous. If you're not with him, then he thinks you're against him, and he's pissed and jealous that I'm translating for someone else.

Mélusine grins at this.

Well, he's not wrong to be jealous.

Jeanne doesn't grin back.

I can't believe I'm alive. She rubs her arms, looks her legs up and down, touches her lips. Everything intact. What happened then? I just don't understand. I was dying. I could feel it. I was so sure.

You look pretty alive to me. The doctors said you just needed some fluids and nutrients and you aren't supposed to drink for a while. Like, a long while.

It wasn't a dream. We were at the Gibeau Orange Julep.

She waits for Mélusine to leave. To tell her she is insane, to get mad. But she is sitting there, deep in thought, considering everything that Jeanne tells her. *She believes me*, Jeanne realises. Ironic, since even now she is not sure she fully believes what Mélusine has told her. She is not sure she believes her story, but she trusts her, which is something different.

Jeanne remembers that she has Yuri's notebook in her purse. For once, she has something on Konstantin. She turns to Mélusine.

Listen, I think I can get rid of him for good, but I need your help. Will you help me?

There is never any question.

I'm in, Mélusine says.

*

The eyes give him away. He's frightened.

Konstantin is sitting on Mélusine's couch. It's a few days after Jeanne left the hospital. With Mélusine's permission, she called and asked him to come over to her place. He came right away, like she knew he would. His hair is still wet, he looks like he ran out straight of the shower. Once Konstantin is inside, the air in Mélusine's apartment seems thinner. He grips the arms of the sofa and waits for her to speak; she savours the role reversal.

I can't believe you tried to kill me.

It was an accident.

An accident where you poisoned my orange julep? Well, I suppose it'll be another accident if some scissors slip and cut your balls off.

This isn't funny, Jean.

Just tell me one thing, Konstantin. You remember that blue vase, in the Museum of Broken Relationships?

What?

Tell me who broke that vase.

Vase? What vase?

Tell me who broke it.

I don't know what the fuck you're talking about, but I've never broken any vase.

I'm not alone this time, Konstantin. So don't fuck with me. I'm not going to warn you again.

Mélusine snarls at him.

Listen to her, Constant Teen. Don't fuck with us.

As a reflex, she clenches her first. It's been years since Mélusine's had to fight for her life, but her body still remembers how.

Sorry, who the hell are you?

Mélusine. Jeanne's amie.

The French form is ambiguous, leaving room for platonic or romantic love. Konstantin's face shifts in understanding, she is a threat.

I know who you are. You're the one who made her crazy, he growls.

No, I didn't 'make' her anything. You're the only one who thinks of her as an object, something you can pick up and put down when you want, something you can control.

You think if I could control my wife I'd be in fucking Montréal right now? I hate this city. I didn't want to chase her here.

She left you. Don't you get it?

He doesn't respond, exhaling deeply and turning his attention to Jeanne.

Involving your girlfriend in our business? You're better than that, Jean.

I'm not better than anything. I'm the worst.

You're not. I still love you, I'm prepared to forgive what you did if you come clean and stop this nonsense right now.

You never loved me. You loved an idea, a projection, a fantasy, I don't know, but you never saw me for me.

That's ridiculous. I did so much for you.

Everything you ever did for me was ultimately for your own benefit.

Fine. Have it your way. I'm the bad guy, I can do nothing right, I deserve to die. You're the one who called me. Why don't you just tell me what you want from me. A cheque? Is that it? A divorce?

It's very simple, Konstantin. I want you to go away. For good. Don't contact me again, don't mention my name around. Pretend I never existed. That shouldn't be so hard for you. You don't need to get revenge on me. You'll live. Ok?

You think I can just ignore this? What a блять you've been, how you've burned through all my accounts? I'm not going to let this go. You owe me. You. Owe. Me.

Jeanne thinks back to what she told the bookstore owner, about how she'd paid for all of her choices. Her laugh comes out cold.

I don't owe you anything. I've given you far more than I ever took.

Ha. That's rich. Jean, you were nothing without me. Nothing.

She wants to yell, she wishes he would call her anything but that, any of her names— John, Jeanne, she hates the way the name sounds curled up, dying in his mouth.

You love that narrative. But have you ever thought about what you were without me? Until I got your work to a wider audience, until I kept house and did all the tedious, boring shit, so that you could have adventures and cheat on me, until I dulled myself so that you could shine that much brighter?

What are you talking about? You think you did me favours? You think anyone in the literary world knows who the fuck you are?

She takes a deep breath, composes herself. Too easy to get sucked into these old arguments with him. She has Mélusine, she has an ally. She has to finish this while she has the chance.

Look, Konstantin, the only thing you need to know is that you either agree to leave me alone, and I never hear from you again, or I'm going to let everyone know your secret.

Mélusine looks up.

Secret?

Yes, exactly what imaginary secrets are you talking about?

You know what I mean. Yuri.

What about him?

You stole his work. After he fucking died. You stole your dead friend's poems.

What are you talking about?

She is choking on tears now. She answers him:

Every word of yours I've ever loved belonged to someone else. I feel so stupid. I fell in love with someone else's writing.

I don't know what you think happened, but obviously —

The fucking notebook, Konstantin. It's in his handwriting. It's dated. You didn't write the poems in your book. He did. Those were his experiences you stole. Sure, you might have changed a line here and there to make it sound like yours. But it's plagiarism. That's why your new poems were shit. They weren't his. After you published all of his material, you had nothing left.

She watches his face closely for any change but sees none. Mélusine, however, stares, mouth agape.

Jeanne can tell she is just as shocked at her as she is at Konstantin. She should've told her sooner.

You can't prove any of this, he says quietly.

She knows this is as much of an admission as she'll ever get out of him. She holds the green notebook above his head. Flips through the pages so he can see the text inside. He opens his mouth again to speak, then seems to think better of it. He looks at the notebook as if it is about to burst into flames.

They're my words, he says finally. Mine.

I don't care at this point if they're yours, his, or God's. Whatever you need to tell yourself. I want to be done with this. I want my notebook back. You're chasing someone you're not even in love with. There's no reason for us to be married anymore. I don't want to see you again, ever.

He is silent for a long time. His breathing is slow, laboured. At last, he looks up at her and says:

Fine. If that's what you want Jeanne.

That's when she knows she has won.

For the first time, he's called her Jeanne.

V. Le Manège

The carnival is magic; a swirl of coloured lights, smoke, and laughter. Soft, wistful music drifts by. The air is singed with the smell of cotton candy, or candy floss, or barbe à papa. The sign at the gate reads: Fun Show Amusement. Léo runs off in the direction of the carousel. Out of all the possible steeds, he picks the hippocampus. Shimmering turquoise scales and a long fish tail. He is definitely the mermaid's son. The women stand on either side of him like sentinels as the ride takes off. Soon he's giggling, holding on to the neck of his horse tightly as he watches the same scenery fly past him again and again.

Jeanne is feeling good, lighter. She's been drinking less and eating more. She is almost done translating Mélusine's manuscript for the bilingual version. She hasn't heard from Konstantin since they confronted him a few months ago. The divorce will be nasty, but at least she mailed her wedding ring to the Museum of Broken Relationships. Maybe one day, she will go and visit. For now, she handles everything one day at a time.

After the first ride, the women realise that Léo can manage by himself. Wanting to get in on the fun, they each choose horses. Mélusine picks a zebra, while Jeanne sits atop a cream-coloured stallion covered in a skin of sleek armour. Wild horse, war horse. Round and round they go, until everything starts to blur in her mind; the horses, shreds of clashing music, screams from the rides, people searching for one another in the crowd. Jeanne is light-headed, dizzy. The next round, they grab one of those booths on the carousel that can seat two side by side. Léo rides just in front of them atop his sea monster. They wave to him, cheering him on as he tries to grab the brass ring. Somewhere around then, Mélusine slips her hand into Jeanne's. Jeanne likes how natural it feels, how she can just sink into this alternate life, comfortable.

Afterwards, they look for food to rot their teeth. Mélusine buys cotton candy, one blue and one pink, and tears pieces off to feed to them. Jeanne feels young again, then suddenly remembers that her childhood was never like this.

Bonjour hiiii!

The carnival barker is trying to get their attention for the ring toss. Léo gives Jeanne and Mélusine a pleading look, and soon he is holding five rings. He throws three, missing by inches each time. He swears in French and gives up. Mélusine tells him to watch his language, but Jeanne sees her crack a smile. She tries her hand at one of the last two rings, before handing the final one to Jeanne. Jeanne closes her eyes and throws. Somehow she makes it, maybe because she wasn't trying. Léo picks the prize, a pink stuffed bat wearing sunglasses, cradling it against his chest.

In Jeanne's purse is a one-way plane ticket to a city she's never been to before, in a country she's never been to before, home to languages she does not speak. She tries not to think about it too much. As Mélusine and her son wait in line for slushies, carefully adorning their skin with glitter stickers, she imagines what it might be like to stay here. To live with them and whoever else, to call herself family, to help raise Léo. In her mind, she can craft a happy ending, a bittersweet one, a tragedy. She can live out all these possible lives at once, always the protagonist.

Mélusine and Léo return with the slushies. She takes her slushie, sips. Her tongue turns blue and she sticks it out at them, the piercing catches the sunlight.

On the way to the exit, they stop by the funhouse mirrors. She watches their bodies transform: long and noodly in one, squat and fat in another. Léo stretches his arms out, testing the boundaries of the magic trick. Jeanne leans in close to Mélusine, so that their lines are almost touching. Glass and bent light. She skims the cool surface of the mirror with her index finger, letting it slide off the edge.

FIN

Acknowledgements

Thank you to Susan Finlay, Nastassja Simensky, Hugh Nicholson of MOIST for reading a proof of *Prétend* and approaching me about publishing a new edition — a translation — as *Jeanne* for UK readers. I am grateful for all its lives and afterlives. Rethinking a book in this way has been a huge challenge, but one I've greatly enjoyed. And of course, a huge thanks to Hugh O'Neil, River Halen, and everyone involved with End of the Line Press for originally publishing the novella *Prétend*.

Thank you to the always lovely Julie Agu for reviewing my French translations, and to Ian Ross Singleton for the Russian translations. Thank you to my family, to my BFF Laura Neuhauser, and to Joey Patchan and Sadie for their love.

About the Author

Arielle Burgdorf is a writer and literary translator from French. Their novella, *Prétend* (sections of which also appear in Jeanne) was published by End of the Line Press in Canada. Prior to this they were a Lambda Literary Emerging Writer Fellow, nominated for two Pushcart Prizes, and have been widely published in Lambda Literary, Electric Literature, Worms, Amsterdam Review, and Full Stop. Currently, Arielle is pursuing a PhD in Literature at UC Santa Cruz focused on queer and feminist writers from Québec.

JEANNE is the third book in MOIST's fourth season. Other titles in the series include *UH HUH HER* by Rachel Cattle and *YOU CAN HAVE IT ALL* by Kathleen Heil.